BE**
DO NOT
BOOK FROM B

Clean out Professor Sh~~~~~~~~~ ~~~~~ drag!
you say. Until you sneak into his workshop—
and check out the gadgets. Whoa! He's got a
huge robot in there. And a really cool pinball
machine.

You're dying to try them all. But look out.
Some of the professor's inventions do *shocking*
things! Can you take it? Will you know what to
do when a Walkman attacks you? And what's
that thing labelled "Loreo"? Do you have the
guts to find out?

Whatever you do—don't push the red button
on that remote control! You've already pushed
it? Oops. Sorry!

You're in control of this scary adventure. You
decide what will happen. And how terrifying the
scares will be!

Start on PAGE 1. Then follow the instructions
at the bottom of each page. You make the
choices.

SO TAKE A DEEP BREATH, CROSS YOUR
FINGERS, AND TURN TO PAGE 1 TO *GIVE
YOURSELF GOOSEBUMPS!*

**READER BEWARE—
YOU CHOOSE THE SCARE!**

Look for more
GIVE YOURSELF GOOSEBUMPS adventures
from R.L. STINE:

Give Yourself Goosebumps

The Creepy Creations of Professor Shock

R.L. Stine

Hippo

Scholastic Children's Books
Commonwealth House, 1–19 New Oxford Street, London WC1A 1NU, UK
a division of Scholastic Ltd
London ~ New York ~ Toronto ~ Sydney ~ Auckland
Mexico City ~ New Delhi ~ Hong Kong

First published in the USA by Scholastic Inc., 1997
First published in the UK by Scholastic Ltd, 2000

ISBN 0 439 01229 5

Typeset by Rowland Phototypesetting Ltd, Bury St Edmunds, Suffolk
Printed by Cox & Wyman Ltd, Reading, Berks.

10 9 8 7 6 5 4 3 2 1

"School's out!" you yell gleefully. Leaning on the handlebars of your bicycle, you gaze at your best friends, Jason and Stacey. "What should we do today?"

Jason and Stacey are twins. Both have blond hair and blue eyes. But that's about the *only* way they're alike.

"Let's ride round the park," Jason suggests.

"BOR-ing!" Stacey responds. "Let's go somewhere new."

As always, you make the decision. "We'll go that way," you say, pointing north out of the park.

You race up the wide boulevard on your bicycles. Soon you're in a part of town you've never seen before.

"I've heard this was the oldest part of the city," Jason says. "Some of the houses go back to pioneer days."

"That one looks like it goes back to the dinosaurs," you joke. You point at a high, crumbling brick wall. All you can see of the house behind it is a rotting roof.

A sign by the front gate says PLEASE COME IN.

You turn to your friends. "Let's check it out," you suggest. You turn back to the gate.

And stop. In shock. Because the sign now says DANGER!

Turn to PAGE 2.

You rub your eyes. Did you read the sign correctly?

Then you see that it's loose. It turns slowly in the wind—back to the side that says PLEASE COME IN.

"Let's go in!" Stacey says excitedly.

"Are you nuts?" Jason cries. "The sign says danger."

As usual, you decide. "I want to see what's inside," you declare. The rusty gate is open a crack. You push it all the way open and enter.

You find yourselves in a weedy garden with grass as high as your knees. Beyond the lawn stands a huge old three-storey house. Paint peels from every wall. The porch sags. Several of the windows are boarded up.

"It looks haunted," Jason says nervously.

Stacey rolls her eyes. "There's no such thing," she responds. "But I bet no one's lived here in a long time."

You step on to the sagging porch and peer in the front window. It's so dirty you can't see anything inside.

Then a strong, bony hand clamps round your wrist.

Go to PAGE 3.

Your heart thuds. A fierce-looking old man is holding your wrist. He's completely bald. A bushy white beard hangs down to his chest. His dark eyes squint behind thick glasses.

"It's about time you got here! I've been waiting all morning. I'm Professor Shock," the old man says. "Are you ready to start work?"

"What do you mean?" you demand, pulling away from him.

Professor Shock frowns. "Aren't you from Acme Cleanup?"

"No," Stacey tells him. "We were riding round and saw your gate was open."

"Oh." Professor Shock seems disappointed. "The people from Acme were supposed to clean my garage," he explains. "But they didn't show up. Why don't I hire you kids? It's not hard work—and I'll pay you fifty dollars."

You glance at the twins. That's a lot of money!

Jason nods eagerly. "Sure! We'll be glad to."

"Wonderful!" Professor Shock replies. "Right this way."

You follow the old man to the back garden. Then you see the garage. And you wonder if you've made a big mistake.

Turn to PAGE 4.

The garage is as big as a barn—and packed with junk. Mouldy old furniture. Rotting cardboard boxes. Piles of rags. A rusted-out car. And that's just in the front part.

"You want us to clean *this* out?" Stacey asks.

"It'll be easy!" Professor Shock says cheerily. He hands you brooms and bin-bags. "I'll check it later. Oh, one thing," he adds. "Whatever you do, don't go in the back room!" He points to a partially open green door at the back of the garage.

"But—" Stacey cries.

Too late. He's gone. You and your friends gaze at the incredible mass of junk. Is the money really worth it?

"Let's get started," you say with a sigh.

You find a wheelbarrow and load piles of old newspapers into it. Stacey pushes a broom in the back of the garage. Jason carries boxes to the front.

"Oh, no!" Stacey suddenly calls. "My ring slipped off my finger! And it rolled right into the back room!"

Follow the ring to PAGE 33.

"Be careful when we *what*?" you shout at the mirror.

Professor Shock's face in the mirror is fuzzy. And his voice is so faint you can barely hear it. You lean in and press your ear against the mirror.

"When you enter the Queen's chambers," the professor croaks, "do *not* touch any of her things. If you do, you'll be lost for ever."

"But what about the mirror?" you demand.

"Gaze into it," the old man says. "It will tell you how—"

ZZZT! His image flares for an instant. Then it's gone—for good.

But it doesn't matter. You know what to do now! You hurry towards the twins.

Hurry to PAGE 16.

"Let's work on the door," you say to the twins.

You glance round. Nothing in the basement but furniture. Well, your teachers always tell you to be creative. . .

You and Jason pick up a wooden coffee-table. Holding it between you, you take off running and slam it against the door like a battering ram. *WHAM!*

The door doesn't budge. But the coffee-table shatters!

You grab a lamp and beat it against the door. Stacey joins you, bashing away with a metal statue.

WHAM! WHAM! Beating on the door is a great way to let off steam. But, unfortunately, it doesn't make the door *open*. You're almost ready to give up.

Then you hear a voice outside.

"Stop that racket!" the voice cries. "I'm coming!"

At last! Someone's heard you! Now you can get out and try to stop the cyborgs.

There's a *click* as the lock pops. The door swings open.

Your eyes widen. Look who's standing outside!

Take a peek on PAGE 38.

You decide to try the green door. It swings open at a touch of your hand. You step through. . .

To another room of mirrors. But these mirrors are all small and square. They cover the walls, the ceiling and the floor, like tiles. You look back at the door you stepped through.

Uh-oh.

There's no sign of it.

There's no way out!

Go to PAGE 62.

You decide to try FAST FORWARD. Maybe it'll speed you up, so you can escape Professor Shock's robot!

You jab your finger down on the FAST FORWARD button.

Every single machine in the workshop clicks on at once. And they all run at supersonic speeds! Lights flicker on and off like strobes. The computer printer spews out paper, hundreds of pages a minute. The power drill spins so fast it starts to smoke. The pinball machine flashes and clangs.

And then everything stops. Just like that.

"What happened?" you demand. Your voice sounds strangely tinny. You reach up to touch your mouth.

CLANG! Hey! Your skin feels . . . metallic.

"Congratulations," Professor Shock says.

You glance at him. And gasp. He's turned silver! Light gleams off his polished head.

He's become a robot!

And so have you!

"You fast-forwarded right through all the stages," Professor Shock tells you. "My plan is now complete. Thank you!"

Welcome to Machine World.

Hope you like heavy metal music!

THE END

"We'd better go after our reflections," you say. "What if they *don't* come back? We can't go through life without them. We've got to catch up!"

You thrust your foot at the mirror. It slides right through! A tingle runs up your leg.

And then you're on the other side.

Stacey and Jason pop through a moment later. The three of you are right in front of Miller's Ice-Cream. The sun is shining. The air is full of familiar scents and sounds.

"We *are* home," Jason says. "This is great!"

You point to the plate-glass shop window. Everything is reflected there—everything but the three of you. It's very creepy.

"We have to get our reflections back," you say firmly. "Come on. They must be in the shop."

But when you enter the ice-cream shop, there's no one there but the cashier. A white ceiling fan circles lazily.

Stacey steps up to the cashier. "Excuse me," she says. "Did three kids just run in here? Three kids who look a lot like us?"

Jason nudges you. "There they are," he whispers, pointing to a big mirror on the right-hand wall.

You run over and peer into the mirror. "HEY!" you shout.

What's all the shouting about? Find out on PAGE 67.

"Okay, let's get Uncle Jack," you tell Stacey and Jason. "We'll just leave Professor Shock here for now."

You run back into the mall and pelt down the stairs to the storage basement. The door is held closed by a thick padlock. But strangely, it's not locked. Jason pulls off the padlock and Uncle Jack steps out.

"Red built a monster robot!" you blurt. "And Professor Shock is taking a nap in the middle of the car park!"

"You don't say," Uncle Jack remarks.

You stare at him. How can he sound so calm? Doesn't he understand what's happening?

Uncle Jack smiles at Jason. "So you managed to give the professor the nerve pinch and put him to sleep. Excellent! Our plan is working perfectly," he tells them.

You feel a sudden chill.

"What plan?" you ask slowly.

Get the details on PAGE 19.

You decide to show the remote to your friends. Why not? You can return it to Professor Shock tomorrow. You stuff the rest of your biscuits into your pocket for later. Then you bike over to Jason and Stacey's house.

The twins are on their back porch, where Jason is building a model plane. You tell them about Professor Shock's gadget.

"You mean it can turn *any* machine on?" Stacey asks.

"No way," Jason sneers. "No remote works on everything."

Jason needs some convincing. You point the remote at his half-made model plane and press one of the black buttons.

The model plane soars into the air!

"Hey!" Jason cries. "How did you do that? That plane doesn't even have a motor!"

You find that you can control the plane's motion by holding down the button. So you make the plane turn. Dip. Roll.

"Cool!" Jason declares. He's convinced.

Then the plane suddenly turns in the air. By itself.

And dives straight at you and the twins!

Go on to PAGE 17.

12

You squeeze through a narrow opening between two tall mirrors. It leads into an entrance hall. You and the twins walk in—and stop, shocked.

The inside of the Palace is made of mirrors too! Everywhere you look, hundreds of reflections of yourself gaze back at you.

"What a strange place!" Stacey exclaims.

"I've never seen so many mirrors," Jason says. "One of these must be the one we're looking for."

"No way!" Stacey disagrees. "They wouldn't keep the Queen's mirror in some lousy entrance hall! It must be in another part of the Palace. I bet it has its own special room."

"We should search in here first," Jason insists.

"It's a waste of time," Stacey retorts.

You sigh. Sometimes you feel like a referee.

"I'll tell you what we're going to do," you say.

If you stay and search for the Queen's mirror in the entrance hall, go to PAGE 49.

If you skip the entrance hall and search the rest of the Palace, turn to PAGE 16.

A tiny beetle clings to a branch of an enormous tree. It has a gigantic, trumpet-shaped mouth.

"*AROOOOOOO!*" the beetle booms.

"*An insect?*" Jason says in disbelief.

You step up, peering at the little insect.

"*AROOOOO!*" it shouts.

Your head vibrates like a gong.

"Why aren't you three in school?" a stern voice demands. You glance up to see a man wearing a badge.

"A policeman!" Stacey cries. "Officer, can you help us find the Palace of Mirrors?"

"The Palace is across the lake," the policeman replies. "But you can't go there now. You kids are supposed to be in school!"

Behind the policeman you can glimpse a wide lake through the trees. Something glitters on the far shore. Is it the Palace?

"Come on," the officer says. "I'll take you to school."

You hesitate. Is it worth trying to explain your problem to the policeman? If he believes you, he might help you. But your story is pretty weird. Maybe you're better off running away and trying to get to the Palace of Mirrors on your own.

If you try to get help from the policeman, turn to PAGE 44.

If you run for the Palace instead, go to PAGE 121.

14

You decide to give the backward answer.

"Seven and eight are fifty-one," you tell the teacher.

"Wrong!" Ms Silver cries in triumph. "Everyone knows that seven and eight make fifteen!"

"But—" you start to protest.

"Arnie gave a correct answer, but you told him he was wrong!" Stacey yells.

"Yeah! You can't have it both ways," Jason adds.

"*Silence!*" Ms Silver screams. "I will not tolerate backchat. Into the closet. All three of you!"

Before you can move, the teacher has your ear in an iron grip. Out of the corner of your eye, you see that she's got Jason's and Stacey's ears pinched together in her other hand. You struggle, but you're no match for Ms Silver.

"Give my regards to the sharks," she sneers. Then she shoves you all through the closet door and slams it.

It's pitch-dark inside. You seem to be sitting in a giant woven basket of some sort. Straw pokes into your back.

"Did she say sharks?" Jason moans.

You never get the chance to answer. Because suddenly there's a deafening *SPRRROINGGGG!* Like a giant rubber band snapping.

And then the three of you are hurtling through the air!

Hurtle on to PAGE 85.

You decide to try the white switch. You love pinball! "Who wants to challenge the pinball wizard?" you call and flip the switch.

Nothing happens. The machine doesn't light up. There's no noise. No flashing bulbs, no *KA-CHING!* Nothing.

"I don't believe it!" you grumble, smacking the machine. You're about to hit it again when you see movement out of the corner of your eye. The green door! It's opening!

Professor Shock! You can't let him find you here!

"Back here!" Stacey whispers. She pulls you and Jason behind the pinball machine. You squeeze in between the machine and an old, dusty mirror lying against the wall.

Your elbow knocks against the mirror. Suddenly, lights begin to flash. Sirens go off. The mirror begins to vibrate.

Horrified, you run your hands over the mirror's frame. How can you turn the thing off?

But soon you stop worrying about that. You've got bigger problems.

A weird, invisible force is sucking you into the mirror!

Turn to PAGE 63.

16

"Stacey's right. We're not going to find the mirror here in the entrance hall," you announce.

"Hah!" Stacey looks triumphant. "Let's go this way!"

She hurries out of the mirrored entrance hall and down a dark, chilly corridor. Jason's right beside her, still arguing. You move fast, trying to keep up.

After a few moments you notice that the floor slants downwards. The twins are several metres ahead of you. Putting on a burst of speed, you catch up with them.

"Guess what?" you begin.

"Who cares?" Jason grumbles. "All I want is to get—"

"Look!" Stacey interrupts. With a gasp, she stops walking. You peek past her shoulder. Then you stop and stare. You have never seen anything like this in your life!

Flip to PAGE 131.

The plane is aiming straight for your head. Eek! You stab your finger at the remote button that controls the plane.

The plane merely picks up speed!

"Duck!" you yell. You and the twins dive off the porch.

KAA-RUNCH! The model plane slams into the side of the house. It's completely wrecked.

Jason turns to you angrily. "Why did you do that?"

"I didn't," you protest. "Really! It wasn't me. It was the remote. I think maybe it has a short circuit."

"You mean you've broken it?" Jason shakes his head. "Professor Shock is going to be really angry."

"Hey, I know!" Stacey breaks in. "Our uncle Jack has an electronics repair shop in the old mall. I bet he can fix it."

"The old mall?" you repeat, a little nervously.

You're not supposed to go there. After the new mall opened, most of the shops in the old mall went out of business. The whole building is going to be torn down next month. It's a dangerous, deserted place.

Still, you'd really like to get the remote checked out before you return it to Professor Shock. . .

"Let's go," you say, and climb back on your bike.

Cycle to PAGE 39.

18

This is the easiest decision you've made all day.

Obviously, you're going to ram Stacey. She's much more fun to play bumper cars with than Jason!

You set the remote down on the dashboard. "Heads up!" you yell and steer straight at Stacey's blue car.

A huge grin spreads across her face. "You asked for it," she shouts. Hunching over the steering wheel, she speeds towards you.

WHAM! You slam into each other, head on. Stacey's car bounces back and spins out of control. The impact makes your little car rock.

And the remote goes flying off the dashboard.

Your jaw drops. Time seems to slow down as the remote spins through the air, end over end. All you can do is stare in horror.

Pick your jaw up off the floor and turn to PAGE 37.

Stacey puts a hand on your shoulder. "Remember how Uncle Jack told you he built Red's circuits?" she asks you.

You don't like the way she's looking at you. "So what?" you say and shrug her hand away.

Jason puts a hand on your other shoulder. "Well, that wasn't quite true," he tells you. "Actually, it's the other way round. Uncle Red's the one who built Uncle Jack."

Uncle Red?

Stacey smiles. "And then Uncle Jack built Jason and me!"

You're suddenly having trouble breathing. "You mean—"

"Yes." Jason nods. "We're cyborgs."

"We used you to steal the remote from Professor Shock. We knew he'd come after it," Uncle Jack explains. "We had to get him somewhere, away from all his gadgets, where we could neutralize him. You see, he's the only person who could have stopped us."

Your legs start to shake. You need to sit down. "You mean all this time, I've been hanging out with cyborgs?" you squeak. "Helping them?"

"Right," Jason says. "As a reward, we're willing to make you one of us. Isn't that great?"

You? A cyborg? A mutant machine monster?

If you can't beat them, join them. After all, they won, in

THE END.

20

Slowly, nervously, you and the twins step out of the lift. The doors swish closed behind you.

You're in a huge room. Steps lead down to a polished white floor. Staring around in wonder, you walk down them.

Giant red numbers are painted all over the floor, which slopes gently downward. Thick blue and yellow pillars sprout up everywhere. Here and there you see what look like archery targets, outlined in neon light. Odd, wedged-shaped swinging gates are also scattered round the room.

"Where are we?" Jason whispers.

"It looks like a fun house!" Stacey exclaims.

You glance up. Hey! The ceiling is made of glass! Through it, you can glimpse an even bigger room—so vast you can't take it all in.

Then, you spot something else. Something unbelievable. Something so terrifying you can't hold back a scream.

AAAAAAAAGHHH! Turn to PAGE 23!

You and the twins dash through the mall, past the abandoned Kiddie Karnival. You find the emergency fire station at the far end of the first level. But the hose is locked behind glass!

"Stand back!" Stacey shouts. Grabbing a loose tile from the floor, she heaves it at the glass. It shatters.

You seize the canvas fire hose and race back the way you came. "Turn on the water!" you shout over your shoulder.

You reach the car park just in time. The monster robot is after Professor Shock! It rolls after him, whacking at him with its giant bulldozer-shovel hands. Behind it, Red works the buttons on the remote control, laughing like a maniac.

The professor staggers round the car park, trying desperately to stay clear of the deadly shovels. He looks exhausted. You know he can't keep running much longer.

Jason and Stacey come up behind you. "Oh, no! Poor Professor," Stacey gasps.

"Hurry!" Professor Shock pants. "Turn the hose on the robot. Try to short-circuit it!"

The hose is too hard to hold alone. Jason and Stacey grab on with you. The three of you aim the water at the giant machine.

Will the professor's plan work?

Who knows? Turn to PAGE 129.

In big, black letters, the sign says:

JUNKYARD

Huh? Isn't that where people throw away old dishwashers and other appliances? Why would the bicycle bring you here?

The bike tears through the gate. Straight towards an enormous junk heap!

You squint. It's hard to see, with the wind in your eyes, but it appears as if the junk heap is moving. Ugh! you think. It must be covered with rats or something!

Without warning, the bike screeches to a stop.

You, however, keep going.

You sail over the handlebars and fly towards the junk heap. Now, at last, you can see it clearly.

It's a squirming, heaving pile of . . . people!

That's right. In this horrible machine world, human beings are useless. Garbage.

Your bike was simply taking out the trash!

THE END

"AAAAAAGHHH!" you scream.

A mountain-sized man is peering through the ceiling at you!

He has a long, white beard. Every hair of it is like a thick rope. The wrinkles on his face are so deep that you could get lost for ever if you fell into one of them. Thick, black-framed glasses make his tremendous eyes look even more huge.

Wait a second! You recognize this giant! It's...

"Professor Shock!" Stacey shrieks.

"Ooohh..." Jason murmurs. And faints.

Your heart races. What's going on? Where are you? And how on earth did Professor Shock get to be so big?

The professor strokes his beard with his enormous hand. Then he reaches down. His hand disappears somewhere to the right of the glass-ceilinged room.

CLING! GA-ZURK! SPROINGGGGG!

You feel a chill. There's something horribly familiar about those clanging noises...

What's Professor Shock up to? Turn to PAGE 74 and see.

24

Stacey has grown! Her arms and legs are like pudgy balloons. But her head has shrunk to the size of an apple!

"What's wrong with you?" you gasp.

"With *me*?" Stacey demands. Her voice is high and squeaky. She sounds like a talking gerbil. "I was about to ask you the same thing! Your head looks like a balloon!"

"You both look like weirdos!" Jason screams.

You glance at him. Then you stare at him. He's become tall and skinny. Really, *really* skinny. His whole body is no thicker than a broomstick. His arms and legs are like pieces of spaghetti. His eyes are two tiny dots in his long, thin head.

You can't help laughing. The twins look so weird! But your laugh booms out as if it's coming through a megaphone. You reach up and touch your face.

You could fit a basketball in your mouth! It's huge! And your head is simply enormous!

It's all too clear what's happened. Going through the fun house mirror has somehow changed your bodies. Now you look like your fun house reflections!

At that moment a bank of lights flashes on, blinding you.

Blink and turn to PAGE 94.

The hideous Queen marches you to a mirrored, revolving door at the end of the room.

"Ow!" you exclaim. Her bony fingers are biting into your flesh!

The Queen positions you in front of the revolving door. Then she gives you a hard shove in the back. You stumble forward.

"Whoa!" you shout as you whirl round and round.

When the door finally stops revolving, you're completely dizzy. You take a few weaving steps and then raise your head and look round.

Wow! You're in a hall of mirrors! Everywhere you turn, you see reflections of yourself. You frown. Your hair looks messy.

No time to worry about that, though. You've got to get out of here and keep searching for the Queen's mirror.

Now, where was that revolving door? You turn to the left.

Your face smiles back at you.

You go right.

There you are again.

Your heart thuds as you realize: you have no idea where the revolving door is. Among all these mirrors, it could take you *years* to find it again. You're stuck. In a hall of mirrors.

And the worst part is, you're having a bad hair day!

THE END

"I'm sorry," you tell Professor Shock. "We didn't mean to come in here. And we didn't mean to make the robot go nuts. It was all an accident!"

"What about the damage?" the old man thunders. "You've caused thousands of dollars' worth of damage!"

You gulp. "I'll work to help pay for it," you offer.

"You'll pay, all right," Professor Shock mutters. He glances round. "Where's my remote control? I left it on my desk."

"You mean this?" Guiltily, you pull the two pieces of the flat, black box from your pocket.

"You've broken it!" the professor screams. "What will I do now?" Then his eyes narrow thoughtfully. "Never mind. I've just figured out what you can do to pay me back. Follow me."

Nervously, you follow the old man out of the garage and into his house. As soon as he opens the door, loud squawks fill your ears.

"In here," Professor Shock shouts above the noise.

You stop and stare. The living room is even stranger than the garage.

See why on PAGE 72.

Screaming, you and the twins plunge downwards.

THUMP! You land on something soft. You sit up and feel your arms and legs. Nothing broken. That's a relief!

Faint light streams in from a window high above your head. You see that you've landed on a big sofa. All around you are other sofas and chairs and beds. All are covered with dust.

"Oh," someone groans. It's Stacey! She landed in one of the armchairs. "My ankle hurts," she complains, rubbing it.

Opposite you, Jason sits up in the middle of the king-sized bed. "Where are we?" he asks in a dazed voice.

"I think we're in the storage basement for one of the mall furniture stores," you say slowly.

You scramble to your feet and make your way to the door at one end of the basement. Locked. Of course. You pound on it. "Help!" you call. "Let us out of here!" But no one answers.

The window is too high to reach. Hmm. Looks as if you'll have to wait until someone comes down here.

Someone will find us soon, you think. They have to move the furniture before they tear down the mall. You'll be all right.

Then you hear a hideous moan.

See who—or what—is moaning on PAGE 41.

The twins are arguing loudly. It's giving you a headache! All you want to do is go home.

"I'm going to try the mirror," you call over their voices. Briskly, you thrust your foot through the glass.

CRACK! CRASH! SMASH! TINKLE! The mirror shatters.

Whoops! Well, at least you've stopped the twins' squabbling.

"Nice move!" Stacey laughs.

"It's bad luck to break a mirror," Jason adds.

Tiny bits of glass rain all around you. They land on your clothes . . . your hair. . . You try to brush them away.

But they seem to be stuck. All over you.

"Help!" Jason cries. "I'm covered with glass!"

Pieces of mirror swirl round the three of you. The ones that land on the floor jump up and clump together.

"Hey!" Stacey shrieks, pointing. "Two pieces of glass just turned into one!"

In shock, you realize that the bits of mirror are rejoining themselves round you and the twins. Trapping you inside.

Then you notice something else. Something worse.

Go on to PAGE 78.

That yell sounded like Jason! You and Stacey dash after him into the back room.

He's struggling in the grip of a tall, red-haired man with a beard. You stare. This guy is almost as big as Deep Voice!

"Leave my brother alone!" Stacey yells.

"What have you done with Uncle Jack?" Jason cries at the same time.

The red-haired man lets Jason go. "Sorry, kid," he says. "I thought you were trying to steal something. Jack's your uncle, huh? My name's Red. I—uh—bought this shop from him."

Jason scowls. "Why didn't Uncle Jack tell us about you?"

Red shrugs. "Maybe he forgot."

You're in a hurry to leave this creepy mall before Deep Voice catches up to you. "Come on," you say to your friends.

"Wait!" Red cries. "I didn't mean to upset you kids. Tell you what. Let me see your remote. I'll fix it for free."

You stare at him. You haven't mentioned the remote to him! How does he know you have it?

Oh, no! Is he after Professor Shock's gadget too?

Turn to PAGE 61.

You decide your best chance is to do as the Queen ordered. So you rub the carving of the turtles until it's shiny and green. Sadly, you put it aside and continue with your work.

A few minutes later, you glance at the pile of carvings. Hey! It's only half as big as it was before!

Afterwards, you're never sure if you really polished all those stone carvings yourself or if some hidden force helped you. All you know is, by the end of the second hour, every single one of the carvings has been buffed until it glows.

You're hanging up the last one when the Queen returns.

"NO!" she screams. "THIS IS ALL WRONG! You did it! You polished all the carvings! Nobody's ever done that before!"

Is she going back on your deal? The idea makes you so angry you forget to be scared. "Well, *I* did," you declare. "And we made an agreement."

"I know, I know," the Queen grumbles. She sighs. "All right, I'll stick to it. First, your friends." She stabs a finger at the ceiling. The carving of the turtles begins to glow green.

POP! A moment later Stacey and Jason stand beside you. You stare at them and rub your eyes. You can barely recognize them!

What has happened to your friends?

Ask them on PAGE 79.

You snatch the remote off your bed and punch frantically at the buttons. Your finger lands on one of the black buttons.

A second later, the awful, blasting music stops.

Silence! You never knew how great it was!

For a while you simply sit there, shaking. Then you examine the Walkman. It looks the same as it always did.

You peer at the remote. That green ray that came out of it. Did it really make your Walkman go crazy?

You cross to the other side of the room and point the remote at the Walkman. Cautiously, you press the button that seemed to turn the Walkman off.

No green ray. But the Walkman blares on instantly. The music is so loud that you can hear it clear over on the other side of the room. Even though it's coming through the earphones!

Quickly, you press the button again. The Walkman shuts off.

You examine the remote more closely. What are all those buttons *for*? Especially that red one. . .

Dare you find out?

Of course you do. Press the red button on PAGE 91.

"Find the what?" you shout. But it's too late. The professor has gone.

The roaring wind stops. You land sprawling on a slick, hard floor. The twins plop down beside you.

"What happened?" Jason cries. "Where are we?"

You gaze round. The room you're in has no doors or windows. The only decorations on the grey walls are two built-in mirrors.

"We came through the mirror," you say slowly. You're trying to stay calm.

"That's impossible," Stacey objects.

"Look around," you order. "There's no other way in."

"And no way out!" Jason wails.

The three of you stare at each other. Impossible as it seems, you're *inside* the mirror.

And you're trapped.

Flip to PAGE 59.

You and Jason hurry to the back of the garage. You glance towards the front. No sign of Professor Shock.

"Come on," you say. "Let's find the ring."

But when you step through the green door, you forget all about Stacey's ring. The room is packed with electronic gadgets and toys! Every shelf and table holds a cool-looking machine. Lights flash. Circuits buzz. A blackboard is covered with mathematical formulae. The walls are plastered with diagrams of machines.

"I bet Professor Shock is an inventor!" Stacey exclaims. "This must be his workshop!"

"What do all these things do?" Jason wonders.

You're studying two huge switches on the back wall. One's red. One's white. From the red switch, a red wire leads to the back of a three-metre-tall copper robot. A white cable from the white switch leads to a high-tech pinball machine. It looks like the coolest game you've ever seen.

You already know you're going to pull one of the switches. The only question is—which switch?

Pull the red switch to the robot on PAGE 35.
Try the white switch to the pinball machine on PAGE 15.

Then you slap your forehead. Of course! The answer is so simple you're embarrassed it took you this long to think of it. You know how to escape the vines and find the sign to the Palace!

"Walk backwards!" you tell the twins.

As fast as you can, you shuffle backwards. The orange vine immediately starts unwinding. You breathe a sigh of relief.

It's hard to move through the thick vines and trees. Shoots and stems grab at your legs and arms. But you keep going. And, as you suspected, the path quickly clears.

In a few moments you arrive at a familiar fork. Ahead of you are two signs. One says LOREO. The other says PLACE OF MIRRORS.

"Let's take the path to the Palace this time," Jason says.

You nod. It's got to be better than the path you've just tried!

Turn to PAGE 109.

You decide to try the red switch. You reach up behind the giant robot and flip the switch to ON.

At first nothing happens. But then the robot's eyes blink open. Red pinpoints of light shine out of them. It swivels its head. Left. Right. Left. Right.

"Whoa. Excellent!" Stacey exclaims.

You think the robot is the coolest thing you've seen in a long time. "Maybe we can make it clean up the garage!" you suggest.

You aren't sure how to control the robot. You try pushing it towards the green door. The metal man's arms wave clumsily in the air. Then it takes a jerky step forward.

"This is great!" Stacey says.

Even Jason agrees, for once. "We won't have to do any work at all now!" He whacks the robot enthusiastically on its copper back as it lumbers by him. "Go to it, pal."

The robot blinks. Gears whir.

Then it spins round and makes a grab for Jason's throat.

"Help! It's gone crazy!" Jason shouts. "Stop it!"

Hurry to PAGE 86.

"Wh-who's there?" you stammer.

"Never mind that. Just give me the professor's remote control," the deep voice growls.

The remote?

How does Deep Voice know about Professor Shock's gadget? Did he follow you to the mall? Your mind races. You don't know!

But you *do* know you can't give up the remote. If Deep Voice wants it so badly, it must be even more powerful than you thought. You've got to get it back to Professor Shock!

"Yaaah!" you shout and shove your bike backward.

CRASH! CLANG! BANG!

"OWWW!" Deep Voice bellows.

"Grab hands and run!" you order the twins.

Holding hands, the three of you stumble forward. You can tell by his heavy footsteps that Deep Voice is close behind you.

Then, dead ahead, doors suddenly swish open. To reveal a small, lighted, wood-panelled room.

A lift!

No time to wonder how it knew you were coming. You dash in. The doors close. The lift starts to rise.

A moment later, an alarm bell rings. The lights go out. And the lift lurches to a stop.

Turn to PAGE 89.

The remote tumbles down. Hits the floor. Bounces once. And then—

CRUNCCCCCHHHHH!

Stacey's blue car rolls over it. And flattens it.

"Oh, no. . ." you groan.

"NO!" someone else screams. Someone with a deep, hollow voice.

You glance up. Red and Deep Voice are both standing by the edge of the bumper car ring, staring in horror.

"You rotten kids!" Red bellows. "You've broken the remote. You've ruined all our plans!"

That's a plus. You still don't know what Red and Deep Voice were up to, but you're sure it was no good. So you're glad that you stopped them.

But on the minus side, now that the remote is broken, you have no way to turn off the bumper cars.

In fact, you're stuck. As the little cars zoom round and round the ring, you realize that they're going far too fast for you to risk jumping out.

Good thing you like bumper cars. Because you're going to be bumping around in this one for a long, long time!

THE END

"What's all the fuss?" a metallic voice grumbles.

It's Professor Shock's robot! And it can talk! Professor Shock is the most brilliant inventor ever, you think.

Uncle Jack pushes past you. "Where's Professor Shock?" he demands. "We need to see him straight away. We must join forces."

"No need," the robot answers. "The battle is already over."

"The battle?" you gasp. "What battle?"

The robot turns its red eyes on you. "The battle between the humans and the cyborgs," it answers. "We won."

"We won!" Stacey cries, clapping her hands. "Did you hear? We won! That's great news!"

You're not so sure. "Uh, by the way . . . which side are you on?" you ask the robot, trying to sound casual.

"The side of the machines, of course," the robot replies. "Our age is just beginning. Now, follow me . . . slaves!"

The Machine Age may be just beginning. But for you humans, this is definitely

THE END.

You, Jason and Stacey ride out to the old mall on the edge of town. As you draw near, you begin to wonder if this was such a good idea. The mall looks even worse than you remembered! Weeds sprout from cracks in the paving. Several of the windows are boarded up.

"Why is your uncle's shop here?" you ask the twins.

"He's trying to sell it and retire," Jason tells you. "But no one wants to buy it. So he's kind of stuck."

"Uncle Jack's shop is on the second floor," Stacey calls over her shoulder. "Let's cut through the car park." She veers down the driveway into the lower level of the car park.

You and Jason follow. Privately, you wish she'd gone *round* the car park. Sometimes you wish Stacey wasn't so fearless.

Like now. It's pitch-dark in the garage. So dark that you have to climb off your bike. You can't ride if you can't see where you're going!

Are Stacey and Jason still with you? "Guys?" you call.

"Here!" Stacey calls. Her voice comes from your left.

"Over here." That's Jason. On your right.

"Behind you," a deep voice says in your ear. Yikes! Who's *that*?

Shh! Tiptoe to PAGE 36.

40

"What are you kids doing?" Professor Shock demands. Dashing to the red switch, he turns it to OFF. A grinding sound, like a dying car engine, comes from the robot. Slowly its arms stop swinging. Its legs stop churning. Its head falls forward and clangs against its copper chest.

An awful silence falls over the room.

You gaze around at the horrible mess. The flat, black box from the desk is lying in two pieces at your feet. Trying not to draw attention to yourself, you pick them up and stuff them in your pocket. Maybe you can fix the box later.

Professor Shock steps towards you. His face is red with anger. "I thought I told you not to come in here!" he growls.

"Let's go!" Stacey cries. She and Jason bolt out of the door.

You really want to follow them. But maybe you ought to apologize instead and offer to help clean things up.

What will it be?

Follow your friends out of the door on PAGE 54.

Apologize and offer to help on PAGE 26.

"D-did you hear that?" Jason asks, his voice shaking.

The moan swells again. Louder.

"There's someone else here!" Stacey cries.

Who? Where? You glance round the shadowy basement.

"It came from over there," Stacey whispers, pointing towards the corner nearest the door. "Come on—we have to investigate!"

You and the twins cautiously approach the corner.

Then you spot two legs. Sticking out from under a bed.

You and the twins stare at one another. Who's under there? Nervously, you bend down and tug on the legs.

A man slides out from under the bed. His hands are bound behind him. A gag is tied tightly over his mouth.

Stacey gasps.

"Uncle Jack!" she cries.

Flip to PAGE 51.

"I agree with Jason," you announce. "Let's wait here for our reflections. They have to come back."

You hope!

Your words were brave enough. But the empty mirror is giving you major creeps. Shivering, you turn your back to it. "I mean, who ever heard of a reflection that could exist on its own?" you go on. "Right, guys?"

There's no answer.

"Guys?" you repeat.

"Uh. . ." Stacey's voice is very faint. When you glance at her, her eyes are like two saucers. She's staring at the mirror.

You spin round.

Yikes!

Turn to PAGE 58.

The copper robot lurches towards you. It's going to take the Universal Remote and give it to Professor Shock. Who is definitely, completely, unquestionably . . . crazy!

You can't let him have the gadget. "No way!" you shout, and dodge behind the desk. The robot clanks after you.

"Why make a fuss?" Professor Shock wants to know. "It'll be *nice* when the world is mechanical. Machines are clean. They work hard. They never ask for days off. They're much better than humans! Don't fight me. Give up the remote."

The robot backs you into a corner. There's no way out. Desperately, you aim the remote at the robot and punch some of the black buttons. A few of the shop machines whir on.

But the robot pays no attention. It keeps coming after you.

You clutch the remote. You won't give it up without a fight!

Then you have an idea.

There are two buttons on the remote that you *haven't* pushed yet. REWIND and FAST FORWARD. They might not do anything useful.

On the other hand, what do you have to lose? Go ahead. Press one!

If you press REWIND, turn to PAGE 100.
If you press FAST FORWARD, go to PAGE 8.

44

You decide to try to talk to the policeman. "Officer, it's like this. We aren't really from this world—" you begin.

The policeman snorts. "Button it, kid. I don't want to hear your tall tales." He hustles you and the twins towards the lake.

You don't argue. The lake is where you want to go anyway.

The policeman shoves you into a rowing-boat and then rows to a small island just offshore. On the island is a red schoolhouse with a bell on the roof. "Last stop," he tells you. "Go on in. And don't let me catch you playing hookey again!"

"But—" Jason tries to say.

The policeman raises his hand. "Get going!"

You and the twins walk through the door into a classroom. Several students sit at desks. In front of a blackboard stands a scowling woman in an old-fashioned long dress.

"Welcome, new students. I'm Ms Silver," she says.

"Actually, we don't belong here," you say. "We're—"

"Of course you belong here," Ms Silver interrupts. "All children belong in school."

"But—"

"Silence!" she orders. "Take seats in the back row and prepare for a task."

Go on to PAGE 56.

"I'll stay on the bike," you decide. The thing is travelling along a definite route, almost as if it's been pre-programmed. Which is pretty creepy. You figure you should stick around and find out where it's going. And why.

The bike zooms down a hill. Faster. Faster! Before long, it's moving so fast the wheels start to give off a high-pitched noise. Almost like a scream.

You clutch the handlebars and hunch down. Wind drags at your hair. Your clothes. It's all you can do to stay on the seat.

You're really scared now. But it's too late to jump off. At this speed, you'd splat on the tarmac like a broken egg!

The bike turns left at a white signboard and then races towards a high, barbed-wire fence. There's a gate dead ahead. It's open.

As you whizz past the white sign, you manage to glimpse what it says.

Uh-oh!

What does the sign say? Read it on PAGE 22.

"You're right!" you call to Stacey. "Split up!"

Stacey veers off to the right. Jason turns to the left. You keep racing straight ahead.

You glance back. The bull is after you! He's so close that you can feel his hot breath on the backs of your legs. His hoofs thunder louder. . . And louder. . .

It looks like the end for you. At least Stacey and Jason are safe, you think. Until Jason streaks past on your left.

A bull just like the one behind you is hot on his heels!

Hearing a scream, you glance to the right.

A third identical bull is chasing Stacey.

Somehow, the bull has split into three! And all three mad bulls are after you and your friends.

Too bad! Splitting up seemed like a good idea. But now you're going to be split for real—by the bull!

THE END

You're fascinated by the mirror showing the country scene. "Let's try this one," you say. "If we don't like what we find, we can always come back."

The twins agree. Trying not to feel silly, you poke your left foot at the glass.

Hey! It goes right through! The glass feels rubbery. It's like walking through a bowl of jelly. Your arms and legs tingle.

And then you're on the other side.

You glance round. You're in a flower-dotted field. Jason and Stacey are beside you. Warm sun pours down. Birds are singing. In the distance, cows munch on grass.

But there's something wrong with the whole scene. . .

"The grass! It's blue!" Jason cries. "And the sky's green!"

He's right! And now that you know what to look for, you notice that the cows are red and yellow, while the flowers are spotted black and white. The colours are reversed. Backward!

"Where are we?" Stacey cries.

"Who cares?" Jason says. "I want to go back." He turns round. Then he gasps.

"The mirror!" he shouts. "Where's the mirror?"

Go to PAGE 60.

48

"Heads up!" you yell as the bike carries you away.

It races down your drive and into the street. Straight for a speeding bus!

You jam on the brakes. Nothing happens.

You try to swerve to the left. But you can't control the handlebars. They turn themselves to the right. The bus's radiator looms in front of you. You stare, frozen in terror.

Then you scrape past the bus. With only centimetres to spare.

Whew!

The bike darts in and out of traffic. It's nerve-racking, but there's nothing you can do to control it. So you hang on and try to ignore the danger while you figure out what's going on.

Could this mechanical madness have anything to do with Professor Shock's remote control? When you pressed that red button, did something happen after all?

You suddenly notice that the bicycle is picking up speed. You're already going so fast that the wind is making your eyes water. If you hit anything, you'll be a goner for sure!

Should you jump off now? Or would you rather stay on and see where the bike takes you?

If you want to get off, jump off the bike on PAGE 69.

If you'd rather not jump, stay on until you reach PAGE 45.

"Jason's right. We should look for the Queen's mirror in this hall before we go on," you say.

You examine the mirrors near you. Some are round. Some are square. Some are shaped like hearts. You peer into each of them. They all seem ordinary to you.

But then, you don't know what a queen's mirror looks like.

"Maybe the Queen's mirror has her name on it," Stacey suggests.

It's an idea. You begin checking the mirrors for names. But the only writing you find says MADE IN TAIWAN.

Then you spot something green glittering in a corner. You step over the mirrors for a closer look. But all you find is a green mirrored door, set back into a nook in the wall.

Hmm. Should you investigate what's behind the green door? Or should you forget it and rejoin your friends?

If you try the door, turn to PAGE 7.
If you rejoin your friends, turn to PAGE 128.

50

Sitting up, you pull the two halves of the box out of your pocket and examine them. One has a single red button on it. The other half has eleven buttons. Nine are black, with mysterious symbols printed on them. The last two are white. They're labelled REWIND and FAST FORWARD.

You twist the pieces in your hands. How do they fit together?

SNAP! The two halves click into place. Wow! There isn't even a crack where the break was. The box looks as good as new. It's clearly some fancy kind of remote control.

Should you return it to Professor Shock? you wonder.

Before you can decide, a green laser beam shoots out from the end of the remote. The end that's pointing towards *you*.

What's going on? Turn to PAGE 57 to find out.

Quickly, the twins rip the gag off Uncle Jack's mouth.

"Stacey! Jason!" he cries. "How did you get here?"

"It's a long story," Stacey replies. As she and Jason untie him, she tells Uncle Jack about finding Red in his shop.

"He told us he'd bought the shop," Jason adds.

"He's lying," Uncle Jack declares. "He came into the shop last night, asking questions about my friend, Professor Shock. But I knew better than to trust him. When I tried to call the police, he tied me up and locked me in here. I've got to get out! I have to stop him before he gets his hands on Shock's new invention, the Universal Remote!"

You wish he hadn't said that. "He—well, he might already have it," you admit. You explain about the remote you took from the Professor's workshop and how Red grabbed it from you. "I didn't know it was an important invention," you finish lamely.

"Oh, no!" Uncle Jack cries. "This is a disaster!"

"What's the big deal?" Jason asks. "It does neat tricks. But it's still only a remote control."

"It's much more than that!" Uncle Jack declares. "In the wrong hands, it's a deadly weapon. And Red's hands are the wrong hands, believe me. You see, Red is a cyborg!"

Turn to PAGE 68.

Better think up a lie! "We came here by accident," you say. "We were just about to leave—"

"LIAR!" the Queen thunders. "I know why you're here! My mirror tells me everything!"

"Then you know we're trying to get back home!" you exclaim. "Please, won't you turn my friends back—"

"Your friends will remain carvings," the Queen says coldly. "But you won't join them. Not yet, anyway. Not as long as you do what I want." She smiles.

It's not a nice smile. "Wh-what do you want?" you ask.

"I told you, my mirror tells me everything," the Queen answers. "Except how beautiful I am. For that, I need you."

"You *want* me to lie to you?" you blurt out.

The Queen scowls. "Are you saying I'm *not* beautiful?"

"Of-of course not, Your Highness," you stammer. You gaze at her hideous, blotchy face. "You're actually, uh, very pretty."

"That's better," the Queen murmurs. She smiles. "Tell me, what do you think of my nose?"

Uh-oh. The Queen wants lies. If you don't keep telling them to her, you'll be turned to stone. This could go on for a long time. A very long time.

To tell the truth, this looks suspiciously like

THE END.

The water of the lake only comes to your knees. You start for the boat.

"This is easy!" Jason marvels.

Too easy? you wonder. You glance nervously round, scanning the water for dark fins. But it's all clear. No sharks.

You've almost reached the boat when Stacey screams.

You whirl round. Something big and black has swooped down from the sky and grabbed her.

Something with fins! And lots of sharp teeth!

"What was that?" Jason shrieks.

You can't believe it! It's a shark. A flying shark!

When you glance up at the sky, your eyes widen in horror. Heading for you are more flying sharks. Hundreds of them!

Then one of the things zooms at you. You duck. But it's no good. Dagger-like teeth close on your body. You're whisked up, up and away. Jason is next to you, screaming horribly.

Too bad! It looks as if this adventure has come to a very fishy

END!

"Wait for me!" you call, dashing after Stacey and Jason. You race past the piles of boxes and old furniture in the garage. You don't even glance at the rusted car and machinery.

Speeding outside, you jump on your bike. The twins are already far down the street. You pedal as fast as you can for your own neighbourhood.

After a few blocks, you glance back. Whew! No sign of Professor Shock. You're home free.

When you reach your house, you grab some biscuits from the kitchen and head upstairs. You feel like relaxing for a while. You slip on your Walkman headphones. Then you pop in your favourite tape and lie down on your bed to listen.

That's when you remember the broken black box in your pocket.

Turn to PAGE 50.

You did it! You escaped!

You and the twins bob in the middle of the lake. On the far side, the Palace gleams in the sun. Coloured light reflects off its shiny sides. It seems to be made entirely of mirrors.

"It's beautiful!" Stacey exclaims.

"So what?" Jason grumbles. "It's probably as crazy as everything else in this backward place."

You've learned your lesson, so you row as hard as you can in the wrong direction. The boat moves swiftly towards the Palace. Soon, with a gentle bump, you land on the shore.

You and the twins climb out of the boat and gaze upwards. The Palace of Mirrors is enormous! The gleaming walls reflect the lake, the trees and the sky.

You made it! Now all you have to do is find the Queen's mirror.

Begin your search on PAGE 12.

56

A test? You and the twins exchange glances. Then, shrugging, you head for the back row. You'll wait and see what happens.

"Arnie!" Ms Silver shouts. A blond, freckled boy stands up. "What is seven times seven?" she asks him.

"Forty-nine," the boy replies.

Ms Silver frowns. "I can't accept that answer! Go and stand in the closet."

Arnie turns pale. "No!" he cries. "Not that!"

"You know the rules!" Ms Silver insists. Grabbing Arnie by the ear, she marches him to a door at the back of the room.

"Please—" he begs. His voice is shaking.

Ms Silver throws open the door. "Enter!" she snaps. She shoves him inside and slams the door behind him.

A moment later there's a long, horrible scream.

Your heart races. What's in that closet? But before you can figure it out, Ms Silver points at you.

"Let's see what our new pupils know," she exclaims. "For your sake, I hope you can do better than Arnie!"

Go on to PAGE 73.

ZZZT! The laser beam bounces off your Walkman.

The music suddenly grows louder.

Quickly, you turn the volume down. But the sound keeps swelling. It's hurting your ears!

You switch the Walkman off.

The music plays on! It blares in your ears, so loud you think your brain will fry!

Dropping the remote, you try to yank the earphones off your head. But they won't budge. It's as if they're glued in place.

"Help!" you cry. But you can't even hear your own voice.

The music is so loud your whole head is vibrating. Your eyes feel as if they're about to pop out. You've got to do something. This is dangerous!

Think! you urge yourself. Your Walkman went crazy right after you put the remote together. Maybe if you break it apart again, the Walkman will leave you alone.

Or maybe you should try pressing one of the remote's buttons.

Better decide quickly—before your brain explodes!

Try to break the remote apart on PAGE 80.
Press one of the buttons on PAGE 31.

A giant, blood-red eye is staring back at you.

It's so big it fills the entire mirror. Its pupil is just a slit, like a cat's eye. And its expression is pure evil.

Jason screams. And screams!

"Don't worry," you manage, though your throat is dry with fear. "It can't get us. It's on the wrong side of the mirror, remember? It's just a reflection. A trick of some kind."

You really hope you're right about that!

"It's getting smaller," Stacey whispers. "I think maybe it's backing away."

You force yourself to study the eye. Stacey's right—it is getting smaller. What a relief! Everything's going to be all right, you think.

Until you notice the giant hand. With clutching, groping fingers and long, talon-like nails.

The hand that's reaching right through the mirror.

Reaching for you!

"I thought you said it couldn't get us!" Jason yells.

The giant hand closes round you. Then it starts to squeeze.

Okay. You were wrong. But don't feel too crushed about it!

THE END

Jason jumps up. "Help! I want out!"

"Hold on!" you call. "Don't panic!"

"There's got to be a way out," Stacey declares.

You stare at the mirrors. An idea is forming in your mind. "If we came in through the mirror, maybe that's the way out too. Maybe we can escape through one of *these* mirrors."

"But which one?" Jason demands.

You study the two mirrors. The one on your right seems ordinary. It reflects you and the twins.

The one on your left is a different story. In fact, you wonder if there's a hidden movie projector in the room. Because the mirror shows a peaceful country meadow full of grazing cows.

Which mirror will you try?

If you choose the one with the country scene, turn to PAGE 47.

If you pick the one that reflects you and the twins, go to PAGE 123.

60

Jason's right. The mirror has vanished!

You *can't* go back to the little room!

"We'll be fine," Stacey declares. "Professor Shock said all we have to do to get out of here is find something."

"But he didn't say *what* we need to find," Jason retorts. "We're trapped. Maybe for ever."

You sure hope Jason's wrong. You stare round. There must be some clue, something that will tell you what to do next.

Then, across the field, you spot a green sign. It looks like a normal road sign—except that there's no road near by.

"Maybe that sign will tell us something," you suggest.

Stacey immediately races towards the sign. You and Jason take off after her. Tall, blue grass tickles your ankles. It feels good to run. Until you realize that something is wrong.

You've been running for several minutes. But—"The sign looks further away than when we started!" you blurt out.

You and your friends stop running and turn to gaze back the way you came. You've definitely covered some ground.

"Weird," Stacey pants.

"Maybe it's an optical illusion," Jason suggests.

Before you can reply, something grunts. Right behind you.

Jump to PAGE 97.

You think you'd better not take any chances.

"Run! Again!" you scream at Stacey and Jason.

The three of you tear out of the back room. Red pounds after you. "Not so fast," he yells. "I want that remote!"

He *is* after the remote! Is he working with Deep Voice? you wonder. But there's no time to think about it now.

You race to the front of the shop and grab the doorknob.

ZAP! A fat blue spark leaps out from the metal.

"Ow!" you yell. The doorknob is electrified!

You face Red. "Let us out!" you demand.

"First give me the remote," he replies.

"Why?" you cry. "What will you do with it?"

"And what did you do with Uncle Jack?" Jason adds.

"Enough questions," Red snarls. He paces slowly towards you.

You gulp. He's huge. He's mean. He looks strong.

"There's a back way out," Jason whispers in your ear.

"Use the remote," Stacey suggests softly in your other ear.

It's up to you! But choose quickly.

If you try to escape out the back, turn to PAGE 71.

If you try to use the remote somehow, go to PAGE 134.

62

"Welcome to the Hall of Ten Thousand Mirrors!" a hollow voice echoes.

"Who are you?" you cry. You spin round to see who is speaking. But all you see is hundreds of your reflections, gazing at you from the small, square mirrors.

"It doesn't matter who I am," the voice responds.

"Could you tell me how to get out of here?" you ask.

"I *could*," the voice says. "But that would spoil all the fun. Find the way out for yourself."

"Let me go!" you demand. "I've never done anything to you. I'm getting tired of being shoved around!"

"Calm down," the voice tells you. "I'll give you a hint. To escape from this room, all you have to do is find the mirror with a tiny red dot in the corner. That mirror will lead you out."

Search out one tiny red dot in all those mirrors? It's impossible! "What if I can't find it?" you ask.

"Then you'll remain here for ever," the voice replies.

"But—" you start to protest.

"Better get started," the voice interrupts. "There are ten thousand mirrors in here."

Quick! Go to PAGE 110.

Wind roars past your ears. It's as if you're caught in a tornado! You can't see your legs any more. They're inside the mirror! You grab the frame and hang on. Invisible forces rip at your fingers, trying to prise them loose.

"Stacey! Jason!" you scream. "Help me!"

But your friends are screaming too. They're being pulled into the mirror with you!

You're inside as far as your neck now. Then a wrinkled face appears, framed by the back legs of the pinball machine. It's Professor Shock! He peers at you.

"Help us!" you shout.

"I can't!" he screams. "I told you to stay away! There's no way out of there unless you find the—"

POP!

Your hands lose their grip. And the professor vanishes.

Let the wind blow you to PAGE 32.

"Turn round!" you shout.

"Huh?" Jason gasps. "Did you happen to notice we're being chased by a raging bull?"

"I think I know how to beat him!" you pant.

"How?" Stacey demands.

"Run towards him!" you exclaim. "We're in a mirror world. Things are backward here—like the colours. So maybe this chase is backward too. Maybe if we run *towards* the bull, we'll get away from him!"

Stacey disagrees. "That's crazy. Let's split up and keep running away. The bull can't chase all three of us!"

Maybe Stacey's plan *is* better than yours. If only you had a little time to think it over.

But you don't. Quick! Make a decision now!

Run towards the bull on PAGE 105.
Split up and keep running away to PAGE 46.

You remember the warning Professor Shock gave you from the mirror. "Wait!" you cry. "Don't touch it!"

"Stacey!" Jason shouts. He grabs her and tries to pull her back.

But it's too late. Stacey touches the rose.

POP! Both your friends vanish. Just like that.

You look round in panic. But there's no sign of them.

They've gone.

Go on to PAGE 82.

You gaze into the mirror, hoping to see the world you came from. The real world.

Instead, you see—nothing.

There is no reflection inside this mirror! Behind the glass, there's just—nothing.

"Creepy!" Stacey mutters. "What kind of mirror is this?"

"A backward mirror," you answer with a sigh. "But maybe we can step through it. Maybe it will take us back home."

"I doubt it," Jason says glumly. "We still haven't found whatever Professor Shock told us to find. But let's try it."

"I don't want to go yet! I want to see the Loreo," Stacey objects. "Come on, let's sit down."

"No! Let's go!" Jason whines.

You're feeling cranky yourself. Should you just give up on the Loreo and try the mirror? Or would you rather wait for the Loreo after all?

Which will it be? Step through the mirror on PAGE 28, or wait for the Loreo on PAGE 125.

"Oh, no! It's happening again!" Stacey cries.

She's right. Once again, your reflections are shrieking in soundless terror. Yours throws up its hands. Stacey's starts to tremble. Jason's puts its hands over its eyes.

Then, just as before, they turn and run away!

"Wait!" you scream. Lunging forward, you dive head first into the big mirror. Jason and Stacey are right behind you.

Your body tingles. Then you tumble out on to the wooden floor of an empty ice-cream shop. A moving shadow makes you look up.

A white ceiling fan circles lazily overhead.

You're in Miller's!

"Not again!" Stacey exclaims.

"It's déjà vu," Jason moans.

This time, the mirror is on the left-hand wall. You peek at your reflection. And as soon as you lock eyes, it happens again. The screaming. The running away.

Finally, you get it.

Your reflection is running away from . . . you!

You don't know why. All you know is, you've got to keep after your reflection until you catch it.

Even if it takes the rest of your life. . .

THE END

You stare at Uncle Jack. Maybe being tied up has made him a little funny in the head! "Red is a *cyborg*?" you repeat.

Yeah, right!

But Uncle Jack nods solemnly. "He's half human, half machine. Professor Shock invented the technology to make cyborgs years ago. I helped. I built Red's circuits. And now he's the leader of a band of rebel cyborgs!"

Uncle Jack is starting to scare you. He sounds completely serious. Could he be telling the truth?

Stacey and Jason appear to be convinced. And they know Uncle Jack better than you do.

"Wh-what do the cyborgs want?" Stacey stammers.

"Power," Uncle Jack replies. "Cyborgs are bigger, stronger and faster than natural humans. They think that makes them better. Red told me about their plan."

He stares at each of you in turn. Leaning forward, he whispers, "They want to make us their slaves!"

Turn to PAGE 81.

You realize you'd better jump off the bike now, while you still can. "Aaahh!" you scream as you throw yourself off the speeding machine.

THUD! You hit the ground rolling. You'll probably have a few bruises, but you decide bruises aren't so terrible.

Standing up, you gaze round. Excellent! By sheer chance, you ended up only a block from Professor Shock's house. Soon he'll put an end to this mechanical nightmare!

You run past spouting garden hoses and whining weed-whackers, straight to Professor Shock's garage. The professor is probably in his workshop. Cleaning up the mess you made!

"Professor Shock?" you call. "Are you here?"

No answer. You walk slowly through the cluttered garage towards the green workshop door. It's closed.

From behind the door comes a whirring sound.

Slowly, carefully, you push the door open. It's hard to see inside, because the lights keep blinking on and off.

"Come in," a voice calls. "I've been expecting you."

Who's been expecting you? Turn to PAGE 98 to find out.

You press your left thumb down on one of the remote buttons.

The lights in the lift blink on. You hear a faint whirring sound.

Slowly, slowly, the lift begins to drop.

"But we want to go *up*," Stacey complains.

"Who cares!" Jason cries. "I just want to get out of here!"

The lift bumps to a stop. Something makes you tuck the remote into your pocket just before the doors slide open.

You're back in the car park.

Someone dressed all in black is standing in front of the lift. Someone huge. This guy makes Shaquille O'Neal look like a midget!

A hat pulled down low hides his face. But you know it must be the person who chased you before. Deep Voice.

He reaches towards you. His black-gloved hand looks big enough to palm a beach ball.

"Give it to me!" he growls.

Go to PAGE 112.

You decide to go for the shop's back door. Maybe you can outfox Red. "Split up," you whisper to the twins.

You duck to the left. Jason lunges to the right. And Stacey dives straight at Red's knees!

"Hey!" the huge man yells. He looks surprised. And furious! "Who-o-oa!" he cries out and topples over backwards.

CRASH! The floor shakes when his body hits it.

"Nice move, Stacey!" you cheer.

The three of you race through the back door, tear down the hall, and clatter downstairs to the mall's ground floor.

You hurry past the old Kiddie Karnival. Your mum used to leave you there to ride the bumper cars while she went shopping. Now the little cars are covered with dust. The poles that connect each car to the power grid have been removed.

Too bad! you think. You used to love those bumper cars.

Stacey suddenly cries out. You stop and turn round.

She's limping and clutching her ankle. "I've twisted it," she explains. "I can't walk!"

"I want that remote!" Red's voice roars from the stairwell.

Uh-oh. He's coming!

Then you have a great idea.

Help Stacey hobble to PAGE 122.

The only furniture in the professor's living room is a big armchair. It's surrounded by dozens of televisions. All are on, their volume cranked up. It's so noisy you can't think!

The professor seats himself on the chair and then turns to you with a smile. "I like to watch all the TV sets at once!" he shouts. "But I hate to get up and change the channels. Since you've broken my remote, you can change them for me!"

"But—" you start to object.

"Get to it!" he orders. "Or do you want to call your parents and tell them what you've done?"

Quickly, you shake your head.

"Good." The professor leans back in his chair. "Change that one to channel 33," he tells you, pointing at one of the TVs. "Then turn the volume up on that one. Then change that one over there to channel 72. Then fix the picture on that one. . ."

You dash round the room, trying to follow his orders.

"Faster!" Professor Shock commands.

There isn't even time to catch your breath! It's awful. You love channel-surfing. But not like this!

Professor Shock might keep watching for ever. But for you, the show's over. It's

THE END.

You gulp. Ms Silver is pointing straight at you. You're on the spot now!

"I don't get it," Jason whispers. "Arnie was right. Seven times seven is forty-nine! Why did she punish him?"

"Don't forget, we're in a backward world. Maybe she wanted a backward answer," Stacey replies.

"Silence!" Ms Silver shrieks. "Now tell me: what is seven plus eight?"

You're starting to sweat. If you don't give Ms Silver the answer she wants, you'll end up in the closet, just like Arnie.

And you know that would be really bad news!

"I'm waiting," Ms Silver snarls.

If you think the best answer is the real answer, fifteen, turn to PAGE 88.

If you think the answer the teacher wants is fifty-one, try PAGE 14.

GUGUGUGUGUGUG! The floor suddenly starts to shake. A giant, silver ball shoots from a tube on your right. It slams into the back wall, bounces off, and hurtles down the sloping floor. Right towards you!

"Look out!" Stacey yells.

"Yipe!" you squeak, and dive to the side.

Just in time. The enormous silver ball rumbles past you and smashes into one of the targets.

DING-DING-DING! Bells ring. The target flashes.

That's when it all falls into place. You know where you are. And you realize it's not Professor Shock who's changed size.

It's you!

Maybe it was the remote. Maybe it was the blue light in the lift. But *something* has made you shrink to the size of a marble. And something has dumped you where you are now—

Inside Professor Shock's pinball machine!

You gaze round frantically for the silver ball. To your relief, it appears to be losing speed.

Then the entire floor heaves up to the left. You lose your balance and tumble to the floor. The silver ball zooms at you.

That's not fair! Professor Shock is tilting!

And you're

FINISHED!

"We've got to find a way to go through the window," you say.

"We could pile some of the furniture up and use it like a ladder," Jason points out.

He's really pretty smart.

Uncle Jack helps you and the twins shove a table underneath the window. You stack an armchair on top of it. Then you balance a stool on top of that. The pile looks very shaky. But it reaches almost to the bottom of the window.

"I'm too big to fit through the window," Uncle Jack tells you. "You kids will have to go through and then come back and unlock the door for me."

You climb up on to the table. Then the chair. Then the stool. The whole pile wobbles. You feel like a circus acrobat.

Very carefully, you slide the small window up. Luckily for you, it isn't painted shut. Grasping the window-sill, you pull yourself through. Into a row of rubbish bins at the back of the employee car park.

It stinks. Yuck.

But you've made it!

Then a cold hand grips your shoulder. "Where do you think you're going?" a voice demands.

See who's got you on PAGE 104.

You stare, frozen in terror, at Red. You're going to run him over with your bumper car! This is terrible!

Red may be evil, but you don't want to flatten him!

At the last second, Red jumps aside. Reaching down, he snatches the remote control off your dashboard.

"Got it!" he grunts.

Oh, no. If only you'd flattened him!

Red's huge fingers dance over the remote control, punching button after button. Your heart sinks right down to your toes. Obviously, he knows exactly how to use the gadget.

A moment later, your bumper car swerves round and zooms out of the ring. You spin the steering wheel. No use. You can't control the car.

Jason and Stacey's cars race along on either side of yours. The three of you are heading straight for a row of lifts.

You start to panic. *Really* panic.

Is Red going to make you crash?

Turn to PAGE 96 for the answer.

You stand on your porch steps, staring. You've walked into a mechanical madhouse!

A lawnmower roars round your lawn, cutting fancy patterns in the grass. No one is pushing it.

Cars weave up and down the street. You peer through the windows. There doesn't appear to be anyone driving them!

WHZZ! WHZZ! An electric can-opener wriggles through the open front door and down the porch steps. Its cord trails behind it. It isn't even plugged in, but somehow it's running!

There are no people in sight. They must all be inside. Hiding from the machines.

You close your eyes and give yourself a pinch on the arm. Can this really be happening? Or are you having a nightmare?

When you open your eyes again, the first thing you see is your bike. Zooming right towards you. The pedals churn—round and round. But there's no one riding it.

Yikes!

No time to move out of the way. Your reflexes take over. Without thinking, you grab the handlebars and jump on.

Ride your bike to PAGE 48.

As the last bits of mirror seal themselves round you, three kids appear in the tent. Right where you were a moment ago. The three new kids gaze into the mirror.

One looks just like Stacey. Another is identical to Jason.

And the third looks exactly like you!

The one that looks like you raises its arm. Your own arm rises at the same moment. You can't seem to stop it.

The kid that looks like Stacey jumps up and down. Beside you, the real Stacey jumps too. The kid that looks like Jason claps his hands. You hear Jason clapping at the same time.

Oh, no. . .

"Thanks!" the kid that looks like you shouts. You feel your own mouth form the word *Thanks*.

"We hated being in the mirror," the one that looks like Stacey says. "Now it's your turn for a while!"

"Like . . . for the rest of your lives!" the Jason-clone adds with a nasty laugh.

You've traded places with your own reflections! Jason was right, you think. It *is* bad luck to break a mirror.

Oh, well. That's the breaks.

THE END

"Stacey!" you cry. "Jason! Is it really you?"

"Of course it's us!" Jason replies.

"But you're so—so clean!" you exclaim. "You both have new haircuts. And new clothes!" Jason and Stacey stare at each other. Then they glance down at their new clothes. "Cool!" Stacey cries. "How did this happen?" Jason asks.

"You got polished," the Queen mutters. "What did you expect?"

You're ready to leave this place. "You promised to let us use your mirror," you remind the Queen. She glares at you, then opens a secret panel in the wall. A round, gold-framed mirror appears. You and the twins rush up to it and gaze in.

"Look!" Stacey cries. "There are words in it!"

You peer at the swirling letters in the glass. You're sure the words are instructions for returning to your own world. There's only one problem. They're in a strange writing.

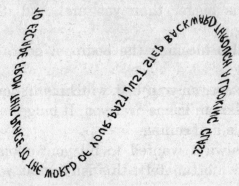

If you can read this secret writing, you know what to do. Turn to PAGE 107.

If you can't read it, go to PAGE 93 for a hint.

80

You grab the remote from your bed where you dropped it. You don't have time to fiddle with the thing. This is an emergency!

As hard as you can, you hurl the remote against your bedroom door. *CRASH!* The black case shatters. Springs pop. Sparks fly.

And the deafening music stops.

Whew! You rip off the earphones and throw the Walkman across the room. It hits the floor next to the remote.

ZAP! A giant yellow spark leaps out of the broken remote control. And into your Walkman.

Uh-oh. Why is the Walkman quivering? you wonder. And why does it look . . . bigger?

In seconds, the awful truth is clear.

Somehow, when that spark hit the Walkman, it made it start growing. You don't know how. Or why. But the thing is expanding in front of your eyes. And expanding! Soon the portable player is bigger than you are! And it's still growing.

It's also blocking the bedroom door. You're trapped.

You cower on your bed, watching in horror as the Walkman looms over you. It bulges against the walls and ceiling.

You always wanted to fill your room with music. Unfortunately, this isn't what you had in mind.

In fact, this is

THE END!

Your heart is beating double time. You're convinced. If Uncle Jack says a group of cyborgs want to make you their slave, you believe him!

Jason is pale. But his scientific mind is at work. "Where does the Universal Remote fit in?" he asks.

"Professor Shock was afraid the cyborgs might turn against us. So he built the Universal Remote to control them," Uncle Jack explains. "Now that they have it, we have no control. But it's worse than that."

Worse? You shudder. What could be worse than a bunch of three-metre super-strongman-machines running wild?

"You see, the remote can control *all* machines," Uncle Jack goes on. "The cyborgs can use it to turn appliances against us. Imagine being attacked by your own TV!"

"Oh, no!" you exclaim. You remember Jason's model plane dive-bombing you. "We have to get the remote back!"

"Right," Uncle Jack agrees. "But first we must break out of this basement."

You gaze round. You could try to reach the window. Which looks awfully small and high up. Or you could try to break down the door. Which looks awfully thick.

Try to wriggle through the window on PAGE 75.

Try to break down the door on PAGE 6.

82

"Stacey!" you cry. "Jason!"

No answer. A moment later you hear footsteps. You whirl around.

A nightmare creature stands right behind you. Blue blotches cover its leathery features. Its hair looks more like filthy grey feathers than hair. It wears a long, shapeless black dress draped with strings of carved stone beads.

The creature opens its mouth, revealing long, pointed yellow teeth. "Who dares trespass in my room?" it demands.

You're shaking in terror. But you must help the twins. "We—we thought this was the Queen's room," you reply.

"I AM THE QUEEN!" the creature thunders.

"*You're* the Queen?" you repeat, shocked.

"This is my chamber," she tells you. "Your friends tried to steal one of my carvings. I punished them!"

"Where—where are they?" you stammer.

The Queen smiles. It's an ugly, ugly smile. She points to the ceiling. You stare up at the hundreds of hanging stone figures. And then you gasp, as you understand what she means.

She's turned the twins into carvings!

"What do you want?" the Queen demands.

Think over your answer. If you decide to tell the truth, turn to PAGE 101.

If you think a lie would be safer, turn to PAGE 52.

You decide to take the remote back to the professor. He must have missed it by now. You don't want him to think you've stolen it!

As you're leaving your room, you hear a sound behind you. You glance back. Your model train is chugging towards you.

And it's off the tracks!

You feel a sudden chill. How did that happen? You were sure you turned the train off before. Quickly, you aim the remote at the train and click. The cars stop moving.

Maybe there's something wrong with the remote. Maybe its insides got scrambled when it fell on the floor of Professor Shock's garage. Maybe there's a short circuit somewhere.

Whatever it is, Professor Shock can probably fix it. You're suddenly in a hurry to get the remote back to him. There's something about it that gives you the creeps.

You rush downstairs. There's a lot of noise coming from the kitchen. It sounds as if your mum is running all her appliances at once. But you don't have time to pop in and find out what's for dinner.

You race out of the front door. And then you screech to a halt.

What in the world is going on?

Turn to PAGE 77.

You decide to give Professor Shock five minutes to nap.

But then the monster robot stirs into life. *VROOM! VROOM!* Its engines roar. It starts rolling towards you on its huge, steamroller feet.

"Yikes!" Jason shrieks. "We're doomed!"

You shake Professor Shock's arm. "Wake up!" you yell. "Tell us what to do! Time is running out!"

The old man's eyes pop open. "Eh? What's that?"

You point a trembling finger at the monster robot.

"Oh, that." Professor Shock frowns. "All right, here's the plan: you kids run to the fire substation in the mall. Turn on the water and bring the fire hose back here."

Water? A fire hose? Does he really think that's going to help against this giant metal menace?

But it's the only plan you have. So you, Stacey and Jason take off.

Hurry! Look for a hose on PAGE 21.

You gaze down, terrified. Water rushes by below you. It's the lake!

There was a giant sling inside the closet, and it shot you right out of the building! Screaming, you and the twins plunge towards the water. The shark-infested water.

SPLOOSH! SPLOOSH! SPLOOSH! You land in a white froth.

You close your eyes, waiting to feel sharks' teeth ripping into your body.

Nothing happens.

You open your eyes. You're bobbing next to a small blue rowing-boat. The policeman's boat! It's empty. It must have come loose and drifted away. What a break!

"Get in!" you order Stacey and Jason. You hold the boat steady while they scramble in. Then they grab your arms and haul you up to join them.

Not a second too soon! As you're crawling over the side of the rowing-boat, Stacey yells, "Shark!"

"Make that 'sharks'!" Jason adds.

You turn round and peer over the side. Sharp black fins circle the boat. These sharks look big. And hungry.

"Too bad, sharks," you call. "We're out of here!"

Go to PAGE 55.

Your eyes widen in horror. The robot is trying to strangle Jason! "Duck!" you shout.

But when Jason ducks out of the way, the robot doesn't seem to notice. Instead it lurches wildly across the room. Bangs into the wall. Spins round. Walks into a chair. Next, it starts knocking things off the tables. Its arms whirl like windmills, smashing into everything that's near them.

The robot is out of control! You wonder if Jason knocked its circuits loose when he whacked it on the back.

"Turn it off!" Stacey screeches.

Snapping out of your horrified daze, you start for the back of the shop. You've got to reach the red switch!

Oh, no! The robot is moving towards Professor Shock's desk. It's stacked with books and complicated charts. A flat, black box with rows of buttons balances atop a pile of papers.

"No!" you shout. Professor Shock will boil you in oil if you let the robot mess up his work. You leap towards the desk. If you can only move the papers out of the way. . .

But the robot is faster. *SMASH! CRASH!* Its metal arm sweeps across the desktop, knocking everything to the floor.

At that moment Professor Shock rushes through the door.

Go to PAGE 40.

You spin round, following Professor Shock's gaze.

The employee car park is full of wrecking equipment. Bulldozers. Steamrollers. Cranes. Wrecking balls.

Standing in the middle of all these machines is a familiar three-metre-tall figure. Red. His fingers fly over the remote.

CLANK! CLANK! The wrecking machines roar into sudden life. Two huge steamrollers position themselves side by side.

"Feet," Professor Shock mutters.

You, Stacey and Jason exchange worried glances. Feet?

A big crane lifts up two bulldozers and sets them on top of the steamrollers. The bulldozers' shovels wave in the air.

"Hands," Professor Shock says, nodding.

TINKLE-LINKLE-LINK! Glass shatters overhead. Glancing up, you spot two wide-screen TVs sailing through the air.

"Eyes," Professor Shock says grimly.

"Eyes?" you echo. You're almost afraid to ask. "Feet? Hands? Wh-what are you talking about, Professor?"

Professor Shock points at the pile of machinery. "Can't you see?" he asks. "Red is using my remote to build a monster robot!"

Oh, no! Do you really want to turn to PAGE 120?

You decide to give the teacher the real answer. But just in case, you whisper a backup plan to the twins.

"What is seven and eight?" Ms Silver demands.

"Fifteen," you reply.

"Wrong!" she shouts. "To the closet!"

"No thanks!" you declare. You give the twins a thumbs-up signal. Then the three of you split up and zoom towards the door.

"Come back!" Ms Silver shouts. "You'll never escape! There are sharks!"

You ignore her and run outside. The Palace gleams on the other side of the lake. A blue rowing-boat bobs at anchor just a little way from the shore.

"Come on," you tell your friends. "We'll wade to the boat and then row to the Palace."

"Wh-what about the sharks?" Jason stammers.

"I can't see any," Stacey says. The three of you gaze into the clear water. There's no sign of sharks.

"Sharks don't live in lakes. Ms Silver was trying to scare us," you declare and wade into the lake.

Go on to PAGE 53.

"We're stuck!" Stacey cries. "The lift was a trap!"

"Help!" Jason yells.

"Stay calm," you say, even though you're starting to panic. You grope in the darkness and press the lift's control buttons.

Nothing happens.

"Can we climb out?" Stacey suggests.

"Too dangerous. Try the remote!" Jason tells you.

Hey! It might work. After all, the lift is a machine. You pull the remote out of your pocket.

You hold it in both hands. So many buttons. You can't tell which ones are which in the dark. Should you press the button under your right thumb? Or the one under your left?

CRRREAKKK!

The lift sways. Then drops a metre!

You all scream.

"Come on!" Stacey urges. "Choose a button now!"

You've got a fifty-fifty chance of getting it right. The odds are even. What about you? Are you even or odd? Count up the letters in your first name.

If you have an odd number of letters, go to PAGE 135.

If you have an even number, turn to PAGE 70.

You turn to Professor Shock in—well, in shock.

"What happened?" you demand.

"Was it the water?" Jason adds. "Did we short out the robot after all?"

"No, I don't think so." Professor Shock strokes his beard thoughtfully. "It was the remote. It stopped working."

"But why? How?" Stacey asks.

"The batteries must have run down," Professor Shock answers.

"The *batteries*?" you sputter. You've just escaped being crushed by a bulldozer, and the human race has just escaped becoming slaves to a cyborg, because the *batteries* ran down?

Professor Shock shrugs. "That's right."

Then he smiles.

"What's so funny?" you want to know.

Professor Shock's smile grows wider. "I was just thinking. . . Good thing I didn't use Supergizers!"

THE END

Taking a deep breath, you punch your finger down on the red button.

The remote lets out a short, high-pitched buzzing sound. But your Walkman doesn't turn on. In fact, as far as you can tell, *nothing* happens.

"What a rip-off," you grumble and press another of the black buttons.

All the lights in the room blink on!

You hit the button again. The lights go off.

A third button controls your TV. A fourth turns your model train on and off. Even though it's made of wood!

Cool, you think. Professor Shock's box is some kind of Super-remote!

That reminds you. The remote *does* belong to Professor Shock. You know you should return it.

But maybe you don't have to return it right this minute. You'd really like to show it to Jason and Stacey. . .

What do you think? If you choose to return the remote to the professor straight away, go to PAGE 83.

If you'd rather show it to the twins first, turn to PAGE 11.

You'll never make it through the gap fast enough to escape the Loreo. "All together!" you shout. "We'll go through the fun house mirror."

"What if it's not that kind of mirror?" Jason asks.

"Then we're monster-meat," Stacey tells him.

The Loreo's hot breath sears the back of your neck. In the fun house mirror, it appears even bigger, more terrifying. Its teeth are the size of shovels. It opens its mouth wide, wider.

It's about to bite your head off!

"One. Two. Three. Geronimo!" you shout and dive straight into the mirror. Jason and Stacey are on either side of you.

To your relief, its surface is soft and rubbery. Your arms and legs tingle as your body passes through.

You hit the ground on the other side.

THUD! THUD! Jason and Stacey land beside you.

You're lying on some kind of wooden platform. "Whew. We're safe!" you exclaim, picking yourself up.

Then you get a good look at Stacey. And you realize you spoke too soon.

Go on to PAGE 24.

93

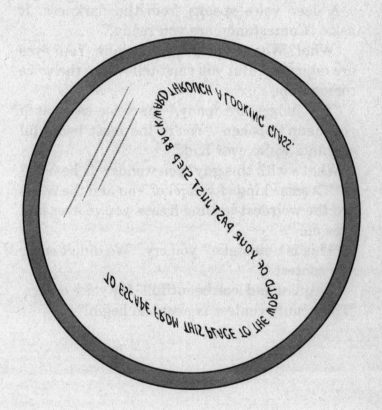

Get the hint? Turn back to PAGE 79.

"What's going on?" Jason cries in panic.

"Where's the door?" Stacey yells.

"Who's there?" you demand.

A deep voice speaks from the darkness. It asks, "Contestants, are you ready?"

"What? We need help!" you exclaim. Your eyes are adjusting. But you can't tell where the voice comes from.

"The judges are ready," the voice says, as if you hadn't spoken. "You're the most beautiful entrants we've ever had."

What's with this guy? you wonder. Is he nuts? Is this some kind of sick joke? You and the twins are the weirdest-looking freaks you've ever laid eyes on.

"This is a mistake!" you cry. "We didn't enter any contest!"

"Be quiet and look beautiful!" the voice orders. "The beauty contest is about to begin!"

Step up to PAGE 103.

Ahead of you, Jason stops so quickly that you plough right into him. Then Stacey ploughs into you. The three of you sprawl on the ground in a pile.

When you untangle yourselves, you see what made Jason stop. There's a fork in the path! On the right branch, a sign says PLACE OF MIRRORS. A sign on the left says LOREO.

"The Palace!" Stacey cries. "Let's go!"

You start to follow her. But then you remember something. "Wait!" you call. "Lots of things in this world are backward. What if the signs are backward too?"

"I see what you mean," Jason exclaims. "The path to the Palace might really be the path to the Loreo."

"What's a Loreo, anyway?" asks Stacey.

Jason shudders. "I hope we don't find out."

"AROOOO!"

"Hurry," Stacey urges. "Pick one of the paths!"

It's up to you. If you think the path labelled PALACE OF MIRRORS will lead to the Palace, turn to PAGE 109.

But if you think the path labelled LOREO will take you to the Palace, go to PAGE 102.

At the very last second, Red pushes another button. Your bumper cars jerk to a halt.

"Get out," Red snarls. "And turn to face me."

You do as he says. Your heart is thundering. What's he up to?

Behind you, the lift doors swish open.

"Step back," Red commands.

You, Stacey and Jason back into the lift.

Hey! There's nothing under your feet. What happened to the floor? Too late, you guess the truth.

The lift's car is missing!

"Help!" you scream.

A moment later, you're falling through blackness.

Plummet to PAGE 27.

Stacey peeks over her shoulder. "Don't look now," she whispers, "but there's a bull behind us. And he's grouchy."

Of course, you spin round at once.

Stacey wasn't joking. The red-and-yellow bull is the biggest you've ever seen. His gleaming horns must be sixty centimetres long. They look even bigger, because he's only three metres away. Pawing the ground. With a nasty glare in his little red eyes.

"Run!" Jason screams.

The three of you pelt across the field. Back the way you just came.

"It's after us," Jason reports, glancing back. "We've got to move faster!"

You pour on even more speed. But when you risk a look over your shoulder, you see that the furious bull is gaining on you.

"The faster we run, the closer it gets!" Stacey gasps.

That doesn't make any sense, you think.

Or does it?

Quick! Run to PAGE 64.

Nervously, you step into the workshop.

Then you breathe a sigh of relief. Standing at the workbench is Professor Shock. He's using a power drill to tighten some screws in his robot's head. That explains the whirring noise.

"Am I glad to see you!" you cry. You pull the remote out of your pocket. "I didn't mean to take this," you explain. "I just didn't want you to know I broke it. But when I put it back together, I think something went wrong. See, I pressed the red button and—"

"Wrong?" Professor Shock interrupts. "What do you mean?"

Boy, he really *is* an absent-minded professor! "Uh—haven't you noticed anything strange?" you ask. "Like the fact that all the machines round here are operating themselves?"

"Oh, that." Professor Shock smiles. "What's wrong with that? That's what my Universal Remote is supposed to do. It's working perfectly! Stage One is complete."

Your mouth falls open. *Stage One?* You stare at the professor in horror. Is he completely crazy?

"You mean . . . you meant all this to happen?" you squeak.

"Of course. Now on to Stage Two," Professor Shock says. He tightens one last screw. Then he turns the robot towards you.

"Robot!" he barks. "Bring me that remote!"

Yikes! Hurry up and turn to PAGE 43!

You decide to ram Jason with your bumper car. He needs to lighten up a little. Maybe this will help.

You place the remote control on the dashboard. Now both your hands are free for the steering wheel.

"Here I come!" you shout and zoom towards Jason's car.

Jason glances up. He frowns. "Cut it out, will you?" he demands. And yanks his steering wheel to the right.

You shoot past, centimetres from the rear of his car. Missed!

He just doesn't know how to have fun. You turn round in your seat. "Come on, Jason, be a sport," you call.

You wonder why Jason and Stacey are both staring at you. And why are their eyes so wide?

You turn round.

Oh, no! A huge, angry figure is standing right in front of your bumper car.

Red! He's caught up with you!

Turn to PAGE 76.

100

You take a deep breath and press the REWIND button.

"Nnn . . . *ON!*" Professor Shock screams.

On? What does he mean? you wonder.

But you don't have time to puzzle it out. The robot is still after you! Its copper fingers reach for the Universal Remote.

And then it steps back. Its hand falls to its side.

It keeps walking. Backward. Back the way it came.

"Etomer eht pu evig!" Professor Shock commands.

Etomer eht pu evig?

Sounds like nonsense. But there's something familiar about it. . .

That's when you finally get it.

"Etomer eht pu evig" is the backward version of "Give up the remote". That's what Professor Shock ordered you to do a minute ago.

The scene is rewinding!

A moment later, *you* start to rewind too.

All the way back to the beginning!

Turn back to PAGE 1.

You're scared. But you decide it's best to tell the truth. "We—we came for your mirror," you stammer.

"My mirror?" the Queen screeches. "Never! No one may have my mirror! I need it. It tells me everything!"

"We only wanted to borrow it," you tell her. "We wanted to look at something through it."

The Queen stares at you in silence for a moment.

This is it, you think. I'm about to become a carving!

She makes a horrible face. Then you realize she's smiling! She begins to laugh. It sounds like a cow choking.

"I like your honesty," she says. "All right, I'll give you a chance to use my mirror. And I'll restore your friends. But you have to earn your chance."

"I'll do whatever you say," you tell her.

"Not so fast!" she warns. "The task I have in mind is difficult. And if you fail. . ." She trails off and gives you that ugly smile again. "Your punishment will be my little surprise."

You gulp. Sounds risky. But your friends need you!

"I'll take the chance," you tell the Queen.

Take your chances on PAGE 126.

102

You choose the path that says LOREO. In this backward world, you're sure you'll find the Palace that way!

"Arooo!" As you hurry along the left-hand path, the hideous sound grows fainter. You relax. Soon you'll reach the Palace. Then, somehow, you'll find the way home.

The problem is, you aren't getting anywhere. After walking for at least an hour, you're still in the woods. You peer ahead. All you can see is—more woods!

"I'm tired," Jason complains.

"I'm thirsty," Stacey adds.

You push through a tangle of leaves. And then you stop.

"Oh, no!" Jason groans.

"You and your bright ideas," Stacey snaps at you.

What's the matter? Find out on PAGE 115.

You hear applause. "Contestant number one!" the voice calls. A spotlight skewers Jason. "Turn round!"

Jason shrugs, then turns round, showing off his weird, tall, skinny body. An unseen audience claps enthusiastically.

"Number two," the voice orders Stacey. "Smile at the crowd."

Stacey smiles with her tiny mouth and waves eagerly. The applause is polite. But it isn't as loud as it was for Jason.

"Number three," the voice booms. A spotlight shines down on you. "Open your mouth. Show the audience your fabulous teeth."

You don't know what else to do, so you obey the voice. Your mouth is so big your lower jaw hits the floor. The audience yells and hoots. They love you!

"And the winner is—contestant number three!" the voice declares.

You've won! It's weird, but you feel almost . . . proud. You wave and bow, blushing all over your enormous face.

Then the stage lights go out. You can finally see the audience. They're fun house freaks, just like you! Their faces and bodies are twisted and warped, bloated and bent.

And every single one of them is gazing adoringly at you.

But don't let it give you a swollen head!

THE END

104

You glance up fearfully.

The person clutching your shoulder is Professor Shock! "I've been looking for you," he says.

Stacey crawls through the window. Jason is right behind her. "Professor!" Stacey exclaims. "What are you doing here?"

"Were you following us?" Jason demands suspiciously.

"Of course I was!" Professor Shock snaps. "I had to get my remote back! Luckily, you kids pushed the red button. That's a homing device. Still, my robot and I have been chasing you all afternoon." He scowls at you. "My robot tells me you threw crumbs in his eyes."

You remember the biscuit crumbs you threw at Deep Voice.

That was Professor Shock's robot?

You start to blush. "I'm sorry I've caused all this trouble," you mumble.

"Well, there's no serious harm done—yet," Professor Shock replies. "Just give it back."

"I can't," you admit. "The cyborgs took it."

"Oh, no!" Professor Shock exclaims. "That's the worst thing that could possibly happen!"

Then his gaze focuses over your shoulder. He gasps.

"I take that back," he murmurs. *"This* is worse."

Go to PAGE 87.

"I know I'm right!" you shout. "Turn round!"

"You're crazy!" Jason wails. But he does what you say.

You spin to face the bull. He's charging straight at you. His horns look as sharp as shish kebab skewers.

What if you're wrong?

Too late to think that way. You've made your choice.

So you sprint *towards* the bull. The twins run on either side of you, yelling.

You blink. Is it your imagination?

Or is the bull a little bit further away?

"Yes!" you shout triumphantly. With every step you take, the bull gets smaller. In a minute, it's a speck in the distance. Then it vanishes completely.

"It worked!" Stacey cries.

"I feel sick," Jason groans.

You laugh. "Let's find that road sign and see if we can go back home again!"

Turn to PAGE 132.

"I want one of those carvings too," you cry and reach for a little onyx guitar.

A single, piercing tone rings in your ears.

Then everything becomes quiet. Very quiet.

You try to glance round. Hey! You can't move your head! In fact, you can't move any part of your body. . .

You can feel yourself swaying. Stone walls glide past your eyes. To and fro. As if you're on a rope swing.

Then a gust of wind spins you round. Your heart skips a beat. You're staring at a life-sized stone carving of a girl. A girl that looks a lot like Stacey. It swings from a thick chain, next to an equally large carving of a red rose.

How'd they get a carving of Stacey? you wonder. And what about that stone rose? Isn't that the same one Stacey was trying to pick? Somehow it got bigger. Or . . . you got smaller.

A chill runs through you. Now you realize what's happened.

You've become one of the carvings in the Queen's chamber!

You catch sight of yourself in a mirror as you swing by it. It's true. There you are, in gorgeous green marble. Forever young—that's nice. But also forever frozen, dangling from a chain— which is not so nice.

Hang in there, kid!

THE END

Now you know the secret of escaping from the mirror world. All you need to do is step backwards through a mirror.

You thank the Queen and rush back to the entrance hall. You and your friends turn your backs on the largest mirror, then step backwards into it. You feel that strange, rubbery feeling again, like walking through jelly.

The next thing you know, you're back in Professor Shock's garage!

You and the twins gaze round. Everything looks normal. The mirror leans against the wall. The big coloured switches are off.

"Let's get out of here!" you exclaim.

You and the twins hurry through the front part of the garage. It's still piled with junk. But you don't feel like doing any more cleaning. You just want to get away from this place!

The front door is open. You can see your bikes, right there in the garden.

Then a dark figure looms in the doorway.

Professor Shock! And he's blocking your way out!

"Oh, no you don't!" he exclaims. "You're not leaving now—not after what you've done!"

He holds up a strange-looking black box with a long tube on one end. He aims the tube at you. "Don't move!" he shouts.

Go to PAGE 116.

108

You aren't in the woods for long before you realize that something is wrong.

Very wrong.

"This doesn't look like the path that we took before," Stacey murmurs. "This path is narrower."

You gaze round. Stacey's right. The path *is* narrower. Because the vines are closing in again!

You swallow hard and keep walking. But soon there's hardly any room to move. And your foot is caught on something.

You glance down to see what it is. A thick, orange vine has wrapped itself round your ankle! The more you tug, the tighter it hugs. And it's climbing your leg. . .

"A tree's just grabbed me!" Stacey cries. "Let's turn back!"

"Back where?" Jason yells. "To the Loreo? Anyway, we can't go back. We can barely even move!"

The vine is past your waist now. Your mind churns frantically. Is this how it will end?

Turn to PAGE 34 to find out.

You and the twins hurry down the path to the Palace. At once you hear the terrifying howl again: "Aroooo!"

"Oh, no!" Stacey cries. "What's making that awful noise?"

"It's following us," Jason declares. He starts to run. You and Stacey tear after him.

"AROOOOO! *AROOOOOO!*"

The sound grows louder and louder. It seems to be coming from everywhere. It fills your head.

"Up there!" Jason cries. He points up ahead.

You screech to a stop as a huge shadow falls across the path. A shadow as tall as a building. With hundreds of arms. And *thousands* of grasping, twitching fingers. From behind the shadow, the noise thunders: "*AROOOOOOO!*"

"Get down!" you whisper. "Maybe we can sneak past it."

You and the twins drop to your bellies and crawl along the path. Then you stop in shock. Now you can see what's casting that horrifying shadow. And what's making that awful sound!

Turn to PAGE 13.

You peer into the nearest mirror. Your face gazes back at you. But no red dots. No dots of any colour.

You examine another mirror. Then another. And another. You see a dot! No, wait—that's a freckle.

You gaze round in despair. And then—you spy something red in a corner of the room.

You rush over to the corner. Leaning against the wall is a bottle of glass cleaner. Next to it is a rag . . . with a tiny red smudge on it.

You pick up the rag and gaze at it in despair.

No wonder you couldn't find the dot. Some-one's cleaned all the mirrors! The red dot has gone!

And you're trapped . . . for ever.

Too bad. *Dot's* the way the cookie crumbles!

THE END

"Go through there!" you shout to the twins. You push Jason through the gap between the tent and the ground. Then you dive for it yourself.

The Loreo pounces, pinning you to the floor. Its mouth is so close you can count every one of its pointed teeth.

"Help!" you scream.

"Go away!" Stacey shouts. She picks up one of the nearby mirrors and smashes it over the Loreo's head.

The Loreo is stunned! Only for a moment. But that's all the time you and Stacey need to squeeze through the gap.

Behind you the Loreo screams in anger. A long tear appears in the side of the tent. Then another. It's trying to claw its way out. It wants its dinner!

You don't wait around. The three of you run as fast as you can away from the woods. In just a moment, you're back among the trees, pushing through vines. You're moving towards the fork that will take you to the Palace of Mirrors.

Or are you?

Go on to PAGE 108.

112

Deep Voice looms over you, his hand out-stretched.

You gulp. Any chance you can bluff your way out of this? "Give *what* to you?" you ask, trying to sound innocent.

"The remote control, dimwit!" Jason cries.

"Jason!" you groan.

"I don't have time to explain," Deep Voice says. "Trust me. You *must* give me Professor Shock's remote!"

"Maybe we *should* trust him," Stacey whispers.

You aren't sure. Maybe it would be better to try to run.

"Hurry! There's no time to lose," Deep Voice insists.

If you give Deep Voice the remote, turn to PAGE 119.

If you'd rather try to run, go to PAGE 124.

And then . . . the monster robot freezes.

Its shovel hands are only centimetres from your head.

"*What?*" Red yells. He holds up the remote and punches buttons furiously.

Nothing happens.

You start to breathe again. Cautiously, you put the hose down and step out from under the shadow of the shovel.

Red is still jabbing at the remote. "Arrgh! I don't believe it!" the cyborg screams. He hurls the remote control at the concrete floor. It smashes into a hundred pieces.

Red sinks to his knees in the middle of the car park. "All my plans . . . my dreams. . ." he wails. "Ruined!"

"I don't believe it!" you say.

The cyborg is crying like a baby!

Professor Shock puts a hand on your shoulder. "Well done," he tells you. "We've been saved!"

Turn to PAGE 90.

114

"Calm down!" the voice cries

You relax. That's Professor Shock's voice. And it's *his* face in the mirror—not you as an old person. What a relief!

"What are you doing in there?" you ask.

"It isn't really me," he answers. "It's my reflection. And it was more trouble than you know to get it to appear."

You don't have time to chat. "Please—get us *out* of here!"

"I can't," the professor answers. "You need the Queen's mirror to escape."

"We know that!" you exclaim. "But we can't find it!"

"It's in one of the Queen's chambers," the professor tells you. "The Queen's chambers are the rooms full of stone carvings. Unfortunately, that's the most dangerous part of the backward world. Be very, very careful when you—"

You wait for the professor to finish his sentence. But his image suddenly begins to flicker. His lips move but you can't hear his voice.

"What?" you yell. "Speak up, Professor!"

Turn to PAGE 5.

You've emerged from the forest into a meadow. In the centre stands a big, yellow-striped tent. A sign over the tent doorway says SEE THE AMAZING LOREO.

The sign on the path wasn't backward after all! The Palace must be the other way!

"Let's start walking back," Jason says grumpily.

"Wait!" Stacey exclaims. "I want to see the Loreo."

You're curious yourself. "Me too," you tell Jason.

You step up to the doorway of the tent. A thin man in a tall black hat holds up his hand to stop you. "Tickets?" he demands.

"Where do we buy them?" you ask.

"Buy them?" the man repeats. He laughs. "What an idea! You don't buy them. I give them to you."

You should have guessed. It's backward!

The man hands each of you a ticket. "Have a seat inside," he says. "The Loreo will appear shortly."

You step through the doorway. The inside of the tent is lined with mirrors. And one of them looks exactly like the mirror you came through to enter this backward world!

You rush up to it. Maybe your problems are over!

Turn to PAGE 66.

You can't believe it! After everything you've been through, this crazy old man has pulled some kind of ray gun on you!

"We're sorry!" you exclaim. "We know we weren't supposed to go in the back room."

"We didn't mean to!" Stacey adds. "Let us go!"

"Please, don't shoot us!" Jason begs.

"Shoot you?" Professor Shock looks annoyed. "But you made it through the mirror world. No one's ever done that! I must capture the moment! Now, just step into the light so I can shoot a couple of pictures. Then you can leave."

You're not sure you heard correctly. Pictures?

"You mean that's a camera?" Stacey asks.

"Yes," the professor replies. "I invented it myself. It's very special." As he talks, he clicks away. "You see, once I've photographed you, you can step into the film negative and find yourself in a negative world. I'm sure you'd love it. . ."

You've heard enough. "Sounds cool, Professor," you say as you push Jason and Stacey towards their bikes. "But we have to go now. Maybe some other day." Maybe some other lifetime!

But as you ride away, Stacey's already starting to say, "It might be fun. Maybe we should come back tomorrow. . ."

"No way!" you shout. "I've had enough. And that's

THE END!"

"What's that noise?" Jason cries.

"I don't know!" you whisper.

"AROOOOO!" The sound is louder now. Closer.

Even Stacey is scared. "Maybe we should go back," she says.

You stop and glance back. Thick vines have grown over the places you've walked. The path has gone! You try to break the vines apart. But they grow back instantly.

You gulp. "We'll have to keep going," you assert.

"*AROOOOOO!*" This time the howl is so loud that the ground shakes. Your eyes dart around fearfully. You can't see anything through these thick vines! What's out there?

"Come on!" Jason cries. He takes off running.

Your heart thudding, you tear after him. Stacey's right behind you.

Quick! Dash to PAGE 95.

118

The carving is of two turtles facing each other. But they aren't ordinary turtles. They have human faces—angry human faces! The turtles appear to be arguing with each other.

You can't help smiling. They look like Jason and Stacey.

Jason and Stacey!

Your heart pounds. You examine the carving closely. The faces *are* your friends' faces. You're sure of it! This is what the Queen transformed your friends into! You've found them!

But what should you do next?

You're tempted to slip the carving in your pocket and make a break for it. If you manage to escape, you'll have the carving with you. And then, somehow, maybe, you'll find a way to turn Jason and Stacey back into real, live kids.

On the other hand, maybe you should polish the carving and hang it up. After all, the Queen said that if you didn't polish *all* the carvings, you'd be punished. Who knows what her powers can do? Maybe you'd better obey her!

Quick! Make a decision. Time is running out!

If you pocket the turtles and make a break for it, turn to PAGE 133.

If you go on with your polishing, turn to PAGE 30.

You bite your lip. "All right," you say. "I'll trust you."

Pulling out the remote, you hand it to Deep Voice. You hope you've done the right thing.

Deep Voice whips out a walkie-talkie. "We're secure!" he barks into it.

The next instant, banks of headlights flash on, blinding you. Dozens of men in suits pour out of parked cars.

"What's going on?" Stacey cries.

"Who are you guys?" Jason demands.

"I'm Agent Jones. We're with the government," Deep Voice replies. "Professor Shock is our top weapons designer." He waves the remote in the air. "You kids have been playing with a very dangerous toy here! All I can say is, thank goodness we got it back before you pushed the red button."

Your heart thuds. "Uh, well, actually. . ." you mumble.

Agent Jones stares at you in horror. "You mean you *did* press the red button? Oh, no! When?"

"About an hour ago." You gulp. "Wh-what does it do?"

Agent Jones shakes his head solemnly. "You don't want to know. Let's just say, we're all doomed. We have only a few seconds left before

THE END."

In the centre of the car park, the monster robot's TV-screen eyes blink on.

It's ready. Ready to crush you!

"What happens now?" Stacey gasps.

"Professor Shock, tell us what to do!" you cry.

"Help us!" Jason begs, grabbing the old man's arm.

"Stop that!" Professor Shock snaps. "I'm trying to think." Closing his eyes, he begins to mumble to himself.

And then he starts to snore.

You can't believe it! You feel like screaming. What a time for the professor to take a nap!

Jason tugs your sleeve. "The professor's too old for this. Let's go and get Uncle Jack," he whispers. "He'll know what to do."

You hesitate. You have to admit, it's a bad sign that Professor Shock has fallen asleep. But still, you believe he's a genius. Maybe this is the way he gets all his ideas.

Maybe you should wait for him to wake up.

If you want to wait for Professor Shock to wake up, turn to PAGE 84.

If you'd rather get Uncle Jack, do it on PAGE 10.

"Run!" you shout. You and the twins take off.

"Stop!" The policeman pounds after you.

The lake is just ahead. A blue rowing-boat bobs at a small dock. "Head for the boat!" you call.

You reach the dock and jump into the boat. A moment later, Stacey jumps in after you.

But where is Jason?

"Help!" Jason shouts. You and Stacey glance back.

Jason has tripped over a rock! The policeman aims a long tube at him. There's a pop. Then a net sails through the air and drops over Jason.

"I've got you now!" the policeman yells.

"Untie the boat!" you instruct Stacey. "I'll help Jason."

You run back to your friend. He's struggling against the net. "Hold still!" you command. Grasping the net, you wrap it more tightly round Jason's body.

"Stop it!" Jason shrieks. "You're making it tighter!"

"Don't squirm," you tell him. Tightening the net is the only way you can think of to make it loose. You pull it even tighter.

The net falls off!

You help Jason up and start running. The policeman is right behind you. You jump into the boat. "Row!" you shout.

Row to PAGE 55.

122

"Get into the bumper cars!" you order the twins.

Jason stares at you. "Are you crazy? We're being chased by a maniac! This is no time for games!" he snaps.

"I know that," you answer impatiently. "Just get in. I have a plan."

Grumbling, Jason climbs into a green bumper car. You help Stacey into a blue one, then you jump into a red one. You pull out Professor Shock's remote and start punching buttons.

When you hit the sixth black button, the bumper cars start to move. It works! You can control them with the remote!

"See? We can ride these out of the mall," you explain.

"Cool!" Stacey says enthusiastically.

"Nice thinking," Jason admits. He starts to steer his car out of the ring.

"Wait a minute," you call. You peer through the gloom to the stairwell. No sign of Red yet.

You know it's crazy. But you're just dying to play bumper cars one more time. Just once, before the mall is torn down and the Kiddie Karnival has gone for ever.

The question is, who should you ram?

If you'd rather bump into Jason, go to PAGE 99.

If you decide to bump into Stacey, turn to PAGE 18.

"It's obvious," you declare. "We'll go through the mirror that shows our own reflections. That'll take us back to the real world."

"Are you sure?" Jason asks anxiously.

You stand in front of the mirror and gaze in. Behind your three reflections is a familiar scene.

"Look!" Stacey exclaims. "It's Miller's."

When you see the ice-cream shop, your last doubts vanish. Miller's is in your neighbourhood. When you step through this mirror, you'll practically be home!

"Let's go!" you urge and step forward.

But as your foot moves towards the mirror, your reflected face twists in terror. Your reflected mouth opens as if you're screaming.

You feel your real face. It seems normal. Your mouth is closed. What's going on?

"Our reflections! They're going crazy!" Jason declares.

"Something is scaring them," Stacey adds. Then she gasps. "Hey, look! They're running away! Quick! Let's go after them!"

"And get caught by whatever is scaring them?" Jason scoffs. "No way! I say we stay right here. They'll come back."

What do *you* think?

If you go after your reflections, turn to PAGE 9.

If you'd rather wait and see what happens, turn to PAGE 42.

Thinking fast, you reach into your pocket.

"Smart choice, kid," Deep Voice tells you.

"I know," you answer—and hurl a handful of crunched-up biscuit crumbs at his face.

Remember? You took the biscuits with you when you left your house. In Scouts' camp, they taught you that it's always a good idea to carry a snack.

Good thing you were paying attention that day!

"Aaaagh! I can't see!" Deep Voice bellows. He stumbles backward, rubbing his eyes.

"Run!" you shout to Jason and Stacey.

The three of you pelt through the car park. Enough light shines from the lift to show you a staircase ahead.

You don't hesitate. You take off up the stairs.

Speed on to PAGE 127.

"We'll wait for the Loreo," you decide. You remember what happened last time you stepped through a mirror. It's too risky to try without knowing what you're doing!

You and Jason seat yourselves. Stacey, of course, has too much energy to stay in one place. She wanders round the tent, peering into all the other mirrors.

"Hey! Look at this, guys," she calls suddenly.

You and Jason cross to where she's staring into a big, strange-looking mirror with a red frame. You peek in.

"Cool!" you exclaim when you glimpse your reflections.

Stacey's head is tiny. Your head is as big as a water melon, while your body is wide, fat and very short. Jason is incredibly tall and skinny and crimped like a crinkle-cut crisp.

"It's a fun house mirror!" Jason cries.

"Maybe we could step through it," Stacey says, her eyes sparkling. "That could be really fun!"

Before you can answer, a loud roar splits the air. It sounds as if a whole pride of lions is approaching!

Go on to PAGE 130.

126

The Queen leads you to another, smaller room. It's piled high with little stone statues. But these aren't shiny and bright, like the ones in the big cave. These simply look like carved rocks.

"These are my new carvings," the Queen tells you. "Polish them! If you finish them in two hours, I'll return your friends to their true forms. I'll also let you use my mirror. But if you fail—look out!"

You gaze at the piles of carvings in panic. There are thousands of them!

The Queen hands you a rag and a can of wax. "Better get started," she tells you, cackling. Then she leaves.

You grab the nearest carving and start rubbing wax over it. Gradually it becomes a deep, glowing blue. You put it aside and grab another.

As quickly as you can, you polish carving after carving. You rub wax on a stone apple, a little house, a woodpecker. All of them grow shiny and beautiful.

But after an hour, you've barely even made a dent in the pile. Biting your lip, you pick up another carving.

You start polishing grimly. Then you notice something very odd about the little statue.

Find out what's so odd on PAGE 118.

You and the twins race up to the second floor of the mall. You glance over your shoulder. Whew! No sign of Deep Voice.

You push through the fire door at the top and stop to rest.

"Who was that guy?" Stacey pants.

"Somebody bad," Jason retorts.

You stare down at the remote in your hand. Whoever Deep Voice was, he was desperate to get the gadget from you. Why? you wonder. All it does is turn things on and off.

Or is there something else you haven't found out?

The twins leads you through the empty, echoing mall to a small shop called JACK'S ELECTRONICS—REPAIRS AND SALES. It's the only shop you've seen so far that isn't boarded up.

"This is Uncle Jack's shop," Stacey announces.

You walk in. The store is filled with televisions, VCRs, radios, telephones, amplifiers and dozens of other machines. But there's no one behind the counter. The silence is eerie.

"Uncle Jack!" Jason calls. He ducks under the counter and vanishes into the back room.

A moment later you hear a yell.

Go to PAGE 29.

128

You decide to finish investigating the entrance hall before you try any doors. You're turning back to rejoin the twins when someone calls your name.

That's funny. The voice is familiar, but it doesn't belong to either of the twins. And it's coming from near by!

You glance round. At first you don't see anything. Then you spot an old, cracked mirror hanging by itself in a dark corner of the doorway. You peer into it.

And gasp.

A hideous, withered old face stares back at you! It's so wrinkled you can hardly see its eyes.

Your heart thunders. There's something familiar about the face. You've seen it before. It reminds you of. . .

Could it be—you? As an old person?

You scream.

Go on to PAGE 114.

The spray of water hits the robot squarely in its TV-screen eyes.

FZZZTT! The giant screens explode. Bits of glass rain down on the paving.

"All right!" You, Jason and Stacey cheer like idiots.

But you've forgotten about Red. Water won't stop *him*. And you've just made him very, very angry.

"You kids are really starting to bug me!" the cyborg bellows. "Time to deal with you once and for all!"

He jabs another button on the remote control.

And the monster robot turns towards *you*.

"Help!' Jason shrieks.

"No!" Stacey cries.

"*Spray!*" you yell at the top of your lungs.

You aim the water at the robot's legs. Its arms. You soak every part of its metal body.

But bulldozers and steamrollers aren't like TVs. They're built to work in the rain. The monster robot keeps coming.

One huge bulldozer shovel looms over your head. The other is poised over Stacey and Jason. You know you're doomed.

"Crush them!" Red cries.

And then—

Then WHAT?? Turn to PAGE 113 to find out.

130

Your stomach knots. "Wh-what's that?" you stammer.

"I bet it's the Loreo," Jason predicts glumly.

"*RRROWWWWWRRRR!*" A huge, tan beast bounds into the tent. It's built like a lion, only bigger. Its toes are tipped with knifelike claws. But the thing's claws aren't nearly as scary as its face. It looks like a furry crocodile, with a pointed snout and sharp, jagged teeth. Hundreds of them. And they're snapping at you.

The ticket man pops his head through the doorway. "Here's the Loreo," he announces cheerfully. "Tah-*dah!*"

"We've seen enough!" you shout. "Take it away!"

"Sorry," he replies. "It's time for the Loreo's dinner."

"What does it eat?" Stacey asks.

The ticket man smiles. "Kids!" he replies.

Stacey gulps. "Could we forget I asked?" she mutters.

The Loreo ambles towards you, drooling. You glance round desperately. There's a gap between the tent and the grass outside. Can you squeeze through before the Loreo pounces? Or should you try to step through the fun house mirror?

Duck through the gap on PAGE 111.
Try the fun house mirror on PAGE 92.

The corridor opens into a big cave. Hanging from the ceiling are hundreds of tiny objects. All are made of carved, polished stones. They twist and turn on their chains, and rainbows of coloured light bounce through the huge room.

"Cool!" Stacey cries. She rushes in. The stone objects tinkle as she passes. You glance up to see a tiny horse hanging on a slender silver chain. It looks just like a real horse. But it's made of polished rock.

"Look at this!" Jason shouts. He points to a tiny blue motorcycle hanging just inside the entrance.

"What a beautiful flower!" Stacey gushes, pointing to a red rose. "It looks so real! I'm going to pick it!"

Did you just get a piece of advice from Professor Shock? If you did, turn to PAGE 65.
If you didn't, turn to PAGE 106.

The sign is as far away as it was. But now you know how to get to it. "All we have to do is walk in the wrong direction," you point out.

"Cool! Let's go," Stacey says.

In a few minutes, you reach the sign. It says

THE PALACE HOLDS THE KEY
DISCOVER THE QUEEN'S MIRROR
AND YOU'LL SOON BE HOME FREE.

An arrow points ahead into a thick, dark forest.

"The Palace?" Stacey exclaims. "The Queen?"

"Who wrote this?" you ask. "What does it mean?"

"I think it's for us," Jason announces. "I think it means that the way home is through this Palace place."

Jason may be quite timid, but he's pretty smart. "Sounds good to me," you declare. "Let's go."

By walking in the opposite direction, you and the twins are soon in the forest. It's a gloomy place. The trees are so thick that hardly any light can get through. Long, slimy, purple-leafed vines choke the path. You hear things moving in the bushes.

"Aroooo!" A loud, deep sound booms somewhere up ahead. It's a cross between a howl and a growl.

Turn to PAGE 117.

Quickly, you slip the turtle carving into your pocket. You look round. The room is empty—who could be watching you? Still, you can't help feeling as though there are eyes on you. Hidden eyes.

Nervously, you reach for another carving and start polishing. Better keep busy in case anyone comes in while you're planning your escape.

Then the door slams open.

"HOW DARE YOU TRY TO STEAL MY CARVING?" the Queen rages. She towers over you. Her blotchy face is twisted in fury.

"I—I didn't mean—" you stammer. "It was just—"

"SILENCE!" the Queen orders. "I thought you were honest. But you betrayed my trust!" She grabs you by the arm. "Now you'll have to be punished!"

Take your punishment on PAGE 25.

Maybe you can turn on all the appliances in the shop and distract Red! You pull the remote out of your pocket.

Bad move.

"I'll take that!" Red says.

Moving unbelievably quickly, he lunges at you. The remote flies out of your hand and skids under the counter.

You and the twins leap towards the counter. Red is faster.

He dives under the counter. A moment later he bobs to his feet. The remote is clutched in his hand.

"Thanks, kids! And goodbye," Red calls. Laughing nastily, he points the remote at the floor beneath your feet.

A trapdoor opens up.

You and the twins hurtle into the darkness below.

Plunge to PAGE 27.

You press a button with your right thumb. Nothing happens.

For a moment, that is.

Then a dim, blue glow fills the lift. As it touches you, you start to tingle all over.

"What's going on?" Stacey cries. "This feels so weird!"

"I don't know," you admit nervously.

The blue light suddenly winks out. The next thing you know, the lift leaps into motion.

Sideways.

The sudden movement knocks you off your feet. The remote flies out of your hand.

"Whoa!" you yell. The lift is travelling so fast that you're plastered against the wall. You can't move!

"Where are we going?" Stacey cries.

"Make it stop!" Jason screams. "Use the remote!"

"I can't. I dropped it!" you shout.

Then, as suddenly as the lift started, it stops. The doors slide open. Light pours in.

Turn to PAGE 20.

Goosebumps

R.L. Stine

Reader beware, you're in for a scare!

These terrifying tales will send shivers up your spine:

Goosebumps

Goosebumps

Reader beware – here's THREE TIMES the scare!

Look out for these bumper GOOSEBUMPS editions. With three spine-tingling stories by R.L. Stine in each book, get ready for three times the thrill … three times the scare … three times the GOOSEBUMPS!

Creatures

The Series With Bite!

Everyone loves animals. The birds in the trees. The dogs
running in the park. That cute little kitten.

But don't get too close. Not until you're sure.
Are they ordinary animals – or are they creatures?

1. Once I Caught a Fish Alive
Paul's special new fish is causing problems.
He wants to get rid of it, but the fish has other ideas...

2. If You Go Down to the Woods
Alex is having serious problems with the school play costumes.
Did that fur coat just move?

3. See How They Run
Jon's next-door neighbour is very weird. In fact,
Jon isn't sure that Frankie is completely human...

4. Who's Been Sitting in My Chair?
Rhoda's cat Opal seems to be terrified ... of a chair!
But then this chair belongs to a very strange cat...

Look out for these new creatures...

5. Atishoo! Atishoo! All Fall Down!
Chocky the mynah bird is a great school pet.
But now he's turning nasty. And you'd better do what he says...

6. Give a Dog a Bone
A statue of a faithful dog sounds really cute. But this
dog is faithful unto death. And beyond...

Creatures – you have been warned!